POWDERHORN PASSAGE

POWDERHORN PASSAGE

Tom Townsend

EAKIN PRESS
Austin, Texas

FIRST EDITION

Published in the United States of America
By Eakin Press, P.O. Box 23069, Austin, Texas 78735

ISBN 0-89015-642-5

LIBRARY OF CONGRESS
Library of Congress Cataloging-in-Publication Data

Townsend, Tom.
    Powderhorn passage / by Tom Townsend.
        p. cm.
    "A sequel to Where the pirates are and Dark ships."
    Summary: Three children once again become involved with Jean Lafitte, thought by many to be dead, in dangerous adventures in Texas.
    ISBN 0-89015-642-5 : $8.95
        1. Lafitte, Jean—Juvenile fiction. 2. Texas—History—To 1846—Fiction. [1. Lafitte, Jean—Fiction.] I. Title.
    PZ7.T666Po   1988
    [Fic]—dc19   88-30192
                                                                        CIP
                                                                        AC

Again, for Janet . . .
Who has made it all come true

Preface

Herein continues the tale of Jem and Raif and Talva.
The story, of course, is fiction, but fiction woven into the
history of the times. The main characters were born in my own imagina-
tion and live only within these pages. Many of the others,
both heroes and villains, lived at the time, although the
adventures they have in this story are also mostly fiction.
The descriptions of places, ships, and events are all
as real as I can make them. To me, this is the craft of
fiction writing—to carry the reader off to adventures
in some other time and place.

1

Polishing boots was hard work, but it was much safer than being chased by pirates, shipwrecked in a storm, or shot at by the Mexican Navy.

Raif Garcia came to this conclusion one hot summer afternoon in Galveston. All of those things had happened to him in just the past two years, so now he figured that he should not have to worry about anything else dangerous coming his way for a very long time.

He was wrong.

Little beads of salty sweat trickled down his dark brown forehead. They ran along his nose and dripped onto the porch of the Tremont Hotel. In spite of the heat, he whistled and popped his polishing cloth as he put a deep, glossy finish on the black boots which rested on his shoeshine box.

Raif was not sure if the customer who was attached to these boots would be a good tipper or not. Although he had learned to tell a great deal about his customers by just looking at them, this one confused him.

The man's accent was very British. His light tan suit, wide-brimmed white hat, and gold watch chain indicated that he had money. But his body did not match his clothes.

There was not an ounce of fat on the man. It occurred to Raif that he looked almost as thin as the long cheroot cigar he held loosely between his fingers as smoke drifted leisurely in gray curls about his head. His face was the color of mahogany wood, deep brown and weathered with tiny lines. An old scar ran across his right cheek. Raif had seen enough scars to know that one of that length and shape had probably been put there by a sword. There were scars on his wrists also, deep reddish-blue streaks that could only have been left by chains. And then there was the earring, a small Spanish gold coin in his left ear, like only a few of the old sailors still wore.

His polishing rag popped one last time, and Raif could see his own face reflected on the boot's toe. "There you are, *Señor*, all finished. You now have the finest boots in all the Republic of Texas."

The stranger stared down his nose and raised one eyebrow slightly. "By Jove, you could be right, lad." There was a twinkle in his blue eyes as he removed a coin from his vest pocket and flipped it in Raif's direction.

"Thank you, *Señor*," Raif answered as he caught a glimpse of two pistols attached to the vest beneath the man's coat. He turned the coin in his hand and saw that it was a Spanish four-*real*. For a moment Raif was shocked by the size of the tip and started to thank him again, but as he looked up, the stranger was just disappearing around the corner of the hotel.

Raif was still admiring his coin when another customer seated himself in front of his shoeshine box. Without looking up, he pocketed his coin, said "Good afternoon, *Señor*," and began applying polish to the new pair of boots.

This customer, he decided, looked older and much poorer. His hair and mustache were silver gray, and he walked with a cane. An old blue seaman's coat hung from his shoulders over baggy trousers of faded sailcloth. A

2

straw hat was pulled low over his eyes. Raif wondered if the man would have enough money to pay for his shine. Then, Raif began to sense something familiar about the man. His very presence seemed to bring back memories of those frightening adventures of the past two years, adventures which Raif would just as soon forget.

Raif was still wondering what it was that was so familiar about him when the old man spoke.

"Hello, Raif," he whispered.

The voice sent chills up Raif's spine and he almost dropped his shoe polish. His eyes got large as he looked up into the face of the man he had met only once a few months before in the far reaches of Double Bayou.

"Mister Lafitte . . . !" Raif gulped. "*Madre Maria*, it is you! But why are you dressed like that and —"

Lafitte's cold, dark eyes shifted from side to side. He touched a finger to his lips. "For now the name is Lauflin, Mr. Jean Lauflin, of St. Louis, Missouri."

"But . . . But what are you doing here? I thought you were —"

"Some things have changed, for the worst, I fear. Can you deliver a note to my son? It is most important."

Raif was too shocked to answer. He managed only to nod as he was handed a small piece of paper.

"I have a room here at the Tremont." Again, Lafitte's eyes shifted nervously. "But I may not be able to stay very long."

Raif's mind ran in circles. This all meant trouble, big trouble, and Raif was not a boy who liked trouble. This was going to be trouble just like he had last year when he found himself sailing off with his best friend Jem to search for buried treasure. Then, just this spring, he had again sailed with Jem and gotten into more trouble than he had ever dreamed of. Both times, the mysterious Jean Lafitte had been involved.

Raif realized that the sooner he found Jem, the sooner it would be over. "I'll find him fast," he said and, sticking

3

the note in his pocket, ran off down the Strand in the direction of McKinnie's Wharf.

Lafitte watched him go and rose slowly. He cast another suspicious glance at three rough-looking men lounging across the street. They looked like sailors, but he knew better. Each one had a cutlass swinging from his belt, two of them were barefoot, and the third wore a pair of woven sandals.

Lafitte left the porch casually and walked back inside the hotel. He passed unnoticed through the crowded lobby and slowly plodded his way up the stairs to the second floor. Just as he reached the top of the stairs, the three sailors from across the street entered the hotel behind him. Three more drifted out of the crowd in the lobby and joined them.

They were an odd mixture of colors and sizes. The three from outside were Spaniards with dark, darting eyes and long, stringy hair. Two others were a deeper shade of brown, probably Carib Indians from the islands of the Caribbean. Their front teeth were filed to points in the tradition of their cannibal ancestors. The last was Oriental, muscle-bound, and almost as wide as he was tall. He was bald except for a long pigtail braided down his back, and he wore only a pair of sailcloth pants and a leather vest.

Together, all six men climbed the stairs cautiously. At the top, they hesitated at a long hallway with doors along both sides. Near the far end, one of those doors was just closing.

"Careful now," one of them whispered. "He is a tricky one."

One of the Caribs spat on the floor. "Don't look like nothin' but an ol' mon ta me." He slipped two big flint-lock pistols from beneath his ragged shirt. "Can't see why they'd be no reward for that gray head."

" 'Nough so's we don't have ta work no more, never," a Spaniard chimed in and slipped his cutlass from its sheath.

4

The Oriental grunted and pushed past them all. "No talk. We kill now."

"Aye, Jongo's got the idea, he 'as," another of the men agreed, and they all followed as Jongo waddled down the hall with his pigtail swinging behind him. He had stopped in front of the door they had just seen close and was about to kick it down when the ominous cocking of two pistols stopped them all in their tracks.

Pale sunlight filtered through the open window at the end of the hall. It reflected off a pair of newly polished boots and two Colt Paterson five-shot revolvers.

"Mexico Thompson!" one of the men hissed. "What are you doing here?"

"Naughty, naughty," the man in the window scolded, pointing with the barrel of one of his revolvers. "I thought I had made it all quite clear that I would be the one who kills Jean Lafitte and that I will do it my own way and in my own time."

"Ol' Firewhiskers ain't gonna like this," a Carib growled with a curled lip which exposed his pointed teeth.

"Undoubtedly, he will not. But that was our arrangement, I believe—"

The time for talk ended before his sentence was finished. "Blast 'em," one of the men said as he raised a double-barreled flintlock pistol. But the Colt revolvers in Mexico Thompson's hands fired first. Long tongues of orange flame belched from both barrels of the Colts as Thompson fired as fast as he could cock and pull the triggers. In less than eight seconds, the guns were empty and a gray haze of powder smoke clouded the hallway.

Blood was spattered along the walls, and a wicked collection of pistols and cutlasses lay among the five dead bodies on the carpet. Only Jongo was not to be seen. In the heat of the first few shots, he had charged through the closed door in front of him, taking the door off its hinges as he went.

For a moment Thompson considered following him and then changed his mind. From the lobby below, there

5

was screaming and shouting. He slipped the Colts back into their holsters, which were built into his vest, and dropped easily to the alley below. He took another moment to dust off his coat and set his hat at a jaunty angle before strolling off toward the street, whistling a merry tune.

2

The sloop *Falcon* cut a white, frothy wake as she tacked her way among the ships anchored in Galveston harbor. At the little boat's helm was thirteen-year-old Jem Dundee, who squinted his eyes against the summer sun as he trimmed the jib. The wind tousled his sandy-colored hair and salt spray cooled his freckled cheeks as he slipped past the stern of the big, inbound steamer *Powderhorn*. He turned slightly and pointed *Falcon*'s bow at a three-masted ship, anchored beyond Snake Point in what was called Bolivar Rhodes.

"Yep, that's the *Boston* all right, up from Santiago with tobacco and bound for London with cotton," Jem said to himself. "Sure wished I was sailin' on her."

Jem had spent a great deal of his life dreaming of going to sea. Uncle Moss Tatum, who owned the sail loft where Jem worked and lived, had been spending a fair amount of his own later life trying to talk him out of going to sea. "Ya can't see now that just by stayin' here, learnin' the trade of makin' sails like I'm tryin' my dangedest ta teach ya," Uncle Moss had argued many times, "why, ya'd be a rich man some day, 'stead of the ragamuffin ya are now."

Most of the *Falcon*'s bow was taken up by a large bundle of new canvas sail, which Jem was delivering out to the *Boston*. He and Uncle Moss had worked late last night and all morning to finish it in time for the *Boston* to sail on the evening tide.

The *Falcon* rounded Snake Point. Jem trimmed his sails again and laid a course for the *Boston*'s bow. He turned his eyes toward the dark ruins of Maison Rouge, the old fortress that stood nearly hidden beneath creeping vines and weeds on a low rise near the point. All that remained now were gray masonry walls and wide stairs which had led to a second floor. Always those ruins had been tied to his own destiny.

Up until last year, Jem had believed he was an orphan with no idea who his parents were or where he came from. His only memory had been living in the little room above the sail loft owned by Moss Tatum and Jeffery Reid.

Uncle Moss knew only that Jem had been brought to Galveston as a baby aboard a ship named the *Laura D*. He had been found, floating on a piece of wreckage near Scorpion Reef off the Yucatan coast. "Ya had that gold locket there around yer neck. We give ya the name 'Dundee' 'cause the *Laura D* was named for a Lady Dundee, an' that's all we know, 'cause they never found out what ship it was what wrecked on the reef."

Last summer everything had changed. It had started when Jem and his friend Raif discovered an old map that would lead them on a couple of long and dangerous adventures far up into Galveston Bay. Before it was all over, they had found buried treasure and Jem had met his father, though only briefly. Now it seemed to Jem that knowing who his father was became a greater burden than not knowing had ever been.

Jem's father was Jean Lafitte, a strange and mysterious figure of whom Jem still knew very little. A few old-timers around Galveston remembered him as a pirate chieftain who built the fortress that now stood in ruins near Snake Point. It was said that the United States Navy accused him of attacking American ships and that he had burned his fortress and sailed away to the Yucatan. Most people believed that Jean Lafitte had died there in a duel with an English officer and was buried somewhere in the Yucatan jungles.

Of course, Jem knew that this was not true, and now he carried the secret, known only to himself, Raif, and two other trusted friends who were now far away.

During the course of his adventures, Jem had also learned that the gold locket with the black falcon on it, which he still wore around his neck, had once belonged to his mother. It had been a symbol of protection, given by his father to only a chosen few.

The white hull of the *Boston* was just ahead of him. Jem stood up at the tiller and shouted, "Ahoy the *Boston*, I got your for'stays'l aboard!"

A sailor moved by the gangway and called toward the quarterdeck, "Lugger's 'longside, Cap'n."

When the *Falcon's* little bowsprit was only inches away from the *Boston's* towering hull, Jem turned her into the wind and brought her neatly alongside. Before the boat had stopped completely, he had scrambled forward and cast his coiled bowline at the gangway. It was caught and made fast, all in one easy motion.

Another line was passed down, and Jem tied it to the bundle of sail. "All right, maties, heave aways now," someone yelled, and the sail was hoisted easily up to the *Boston's* deck.

"Cap'n says he's got some letters ta be mailed," the same voice called down to Jem. "Come aboard and he'll fetch 'em fur ya."

Jem nodded his agreement. He had hoped for an invitation since any chance to look around a sailing ship was a real treat. In fact, the only thing about sailmaking that he liked was getting to see a lot of different ships.

9

He quickly dropped *Falcon*'s sails, checked to make sure she was riding safely away from the *Boston*'s hull, and jumped for the dangling rope ladder that led to her gangway.

The captain, a salty-looking old gentleman with bushy whiskers and a long pipe, smiled at Jem as he approached the quarterdeck. He handed over a large, canvas envelope addressed to the postmaster at Galveston. "Thank you, lad. There's a few letters home the crew would like mailed, if you please."

"Yes, sir," Jem answered as he took the envelope.

"Oh yes, I almost forgot," the captain added, removing a newspaper from his coat and handing it to Jem. "The sheriff wanted me to leave this with him so he could have some hand bills printed up."

Jem took the paper and began to read. It was a New Orleans newspaper and across the front page was printed in bold letters:

Wanted For Suspicion Of Piracy

A vessel fitting the description of the former Texas Navy schooner-of-war *San Antonio*, which was reported lost at sea in September of 1842, has recently been sighted off the coast of Cuba and is suspected of being responsible for several recent acts of piracy in those waters.

It has been reported that she may have been taken over by a mutinous crew and is now under the command of two known pirates, Juan Fuerate (alias Johnny Firewhiskers) and Mexico Thompson (formerly of both the English and Mexican Navies). Both of these villains are also said to have been associates of the late Pirate King, Jean Lafitte, formerly of this city and later Galveston. It is from him, no doubt, that they learned their black trade.

Jem read the last line with dread. His ears burned with anger. He wanted to say that his father was no pirate, but he caught himself and was silent.

"Chased me off Isla Contoy, she did, but I slipped away from 'em in the dark. Some others weren't so lucky, I hear," the captain added and puffed on his pipe.

Suddenly, Jem did not care much about looking around the *Boston*. "Thank you, sir, and have a safe passage," he said quietly as he added the newspaper to the big envelope. He climbed back down to the waiting *Falcon* and, as soon as her sails were hoisted, cast off and headed back for the harbor.

A pair of gray dolphins played beside the *Falcon*, riding the bow wave and diving back and forth beneath the keel. Jem always marveled at these strange, friendly creatures who breathed through a blowhole behind their heads. They made low, murmuring sounds as they breathed, and little fountains of water sprayed up from the blowholes as they sliced easily through the water.

Halfway across Bolivar Rhodes, he opened the envelope again and reread the newspaper article. Jem remembered the Texas Navy schooner *San Antonio* very well. He had helped cut new sails for her while she was stationed at the Navy Yard Pier in Galveston. That, he believed, must have been just two years ago, in June or July of 1842, just before she sailed from Galveston for the Yucatan and vanished.

Far in the distance, Jem could see the masts of all that was now left of the Texas Navy. Ever since last summer, the ships had been laid up. Several attempts had been made by the government to sell them. Only last week most of the charts, lanterns, and lumber had been auctioned off. Jem had also heard that the navy's 200 five-shot Colt revolvers were about to be shipped to the Texas Rangers somewhere far in the west.

None of this made a whole lot of sense to Jem, but then, politics never did. Jem knew all too well how much Mexico still wanted to recapture Texas, and it seemed certain that, sooner or later, there would have to be another war. Apparently, it was going to be a war which Texas would have to fight without her navy.

11

The steamer *Powderhorn* had already nosed in alongside the Morgan Line Wharf when Jem turned the *Falcon* to approach one of the adjoining piers. He was still fifty yards away when he heard someone yelling in Spanish. His best friend, Raif, was at the end of the pier, jumping up and down and waving his arms.

"Uh-oh," Jem sighed, "there must be some big trouble 'cause Raif don't ever speak Spanish 'cept when he's either scared to death or awful mad."

3

"*Andale pronto, pronto*! Hurry up, Jem! Come on!"
Raif was shouting in a mixture of Spanish and English,
which was most unusual for Raif. Jem cast him *Falcon*'s
bowline and then quickly dropped his sails as Raif continued to rant and rave.

"Slow down, Raif, what the heck's happened?" Jem
demanded as he laid the canvas envelope full of letters
onto the pier and climbed up.

"At the hotel, *mi amigo*! I was just coming to get
you when all of a sudden it sounded like everybody up-
stairs was shooting each other all to little pieces."

Jem looked puzzled. "Yeah, so what happened?"

"I don't know! I was coming to get you."

"Oh," Jem answered, growing more confused with
each sentence. "But what were you comin' ta get me for?"

Raif never slowed down. "What do you mean, why
was I coming here to get you? I was coming to give you
this note."

"What note?"

For a moment Raif looked blank and then began fum-
bling through his pockets. "Let me see here, it is in my

13

pocket somewhere, that's where I put it just after I read it so I could not possibly lose it."

"Well, heck, if you read it, just tell me what it said."

"Oh, okay, it was just a room number at the Tremont. I think it was 211 or 213, maybe."

"Dang it all, Raif, will you just slow down and start at the beginning?"

"Okay, maybe that is best," Raif agreed and took a deep breath. "It all started while I was shining your father's boots, except I did not realize at first it was him because he was dressed like an old sailor and—"

"He's here!" Now Jem was yelling. "Come on, let's go! Where is he?"

"That's what I don't know. Just as I was leaving there was a whole bunch of shooting in the hotel. . . . Hey Jem, wait for me!"

Jem was already running down the pier. His mind swirled as he ran. Why was his father here now? It did not make any sense. He remembered the night just a few months ago when they had parted company near Rollover Pass. His father's ship, the *Pride*, was a darkened silhouette against the night sky. He had pointed to Jem's locket and said, "Keep it close. As you have seen, there are still some who know its meaning."

"Will I ever see you again?" Jem had asked, fighting back his tears.

"In my heart, I feel that there will be a time for us someday — someday when all of the wars are fought and deeds are done." Then, as the *Pride*'s longboat pulled toward the shore, he had extended his hand and Jem shook it. "Farewell, my son, we shall meet again." Now, suddenly, he was back in Galveston. And as usual, trouble had come with him.

A huge crowd was gathered in front of the Tremont Hotel when Jem came running up, with Raif still almost half a block behind. Without slowing down much, Jem ducked and pushed his way through, under and around

14

the crowd. He was almost to the front door when he was grabbed by the collar and brought to a sudden halt.

"Boy, where in tarnation do you think you're going?" Jem looked up into the frowning face of Sheriff Smythe and tried to catch his breath.

"Heard there was some shootin'," Jem panted just as Raif came puffing up behind him.

"Well, you heard right, just like all these other folks did. Now you get on out of here. I got six dead men up there. Everything is such a mess, I can't figure out who killed who."

Jem had no choice but to back up and watch as, one by one, the bodies were carried out, covered with sheets.

"Must have been shot up real bad for the sheriff to cover them up before he had them moved," someone in the crowd remarked as one of the blood-stained sheets was carried by.

"I heard there wasn't any of 'em survived. They all shot each other," another voice chimed in. Similar comments followed, and a couple of women fainted before all six bodies were carried off. Jem began to feel sick. Some of the crowd followed the bodies as they were carried down the street to the funeral parlor. Others were still milling around in front of the hotel.

Sheriff Smythe again appeared at the front door. "All right, folks, the show's all over. Go on about your business now. There's nothing else to see here."

Jem took Raif by the arm and led him a little way away from the rest of the milling crowd. "We gotta get a look at those bodies," he said.

"I don't want to look at no bodies," Raif protested, pulling away. "I don't like dead people, especially ones who have been all shot up."

Jem's eyes dropped to the street. "I gotta know if my father is one of 'em."

Raif took a deep breath and nodded his head sadly. "Yes, my friend. I guess we do."

"And we gotta do it in secret," Jem added, "so no one'll figure out what we're lookin' for."

"How are we going to do that?" Raif asked. He was already dreading what the answer would be.

"They'll bury 'em tomorrow, so I reckon we got to sneak into the funeral parlor tonight."

Raif put out his hands and took a couple of steps backward. "Hey, wait a minute now. I do not want to go into there in the middle of the night with all those spooky old dead people."

"Neither do I, but I gotta find out if he's all right."

There was nothing more that could be done until well after dark. Raif said that he would keep an eye on things and went back to polishing shoes on the porch of the hotel. Jem felt all mixed up inside, but he forced himself to stay busy. He took the package of letters from the *Boston* to the post office and then dropped off the newspaper at the sheriff's office.

Sheriff Smythe looked busy, but he took time to read the article. "Umph," he said when he finished. "Mexico Thompson, they say. I figured he'd been dead a long time by now."

"You know about him?" Jem asked cautiously.

Smythe nodded. "There's still a few folks along this coast who curse the name of Captain Thomas M. Thompson and the Mexican frigate *Correo de Mejico*."

"I ain't never heard of 'em," Jem continued to pry. "Says there, he sailed with Jean Lafitte."

The sheriff shrugged his shoulders. "I wouldn't know about that. But back just before the revolution, Thompson was a captain in the Mexican Navy. Took ships all up and down this coast. He was a strange one all right."

Smythe fiddled with his mustache and continued. "Story goes, he changed sides once, helped some Texas sailors escape from a Mexican prison. 'Sposed to have come back to Texas once, using a different name, but folks found out who he really was. Last anybody ever heard, he went back to Mexico. Like I say, figured he be long dead and buried by now."

Smythe folded up the paper and let it drop onto his desk. "Don't have much time right now to worry about pirates down in the Caribbean," he grumbled. "I swear, these killings here couldn't come at a worse time, what with them 200 newfangled Colt pistols being shipped on the *Powderhorn* tomorrow and all my deputies busy guarding them."

"What's so special 'bout a couple of hundred pistols?"

"Special?" Smythe stared at him. "They're special because they shoot five times, just as fast as you can cock 'em and pull the triggers. That's what's special about 'em. They are just about the only ones like that ever been made. A man with two of them is worth ten men in a close fight."

He spit into a brass spittoon in the corner. "Danged fool politicians went and laid up the whole blasted navy, paid off the sailors, and now I'm supposed to keep their guns from gettin' stole."

Jem could see that there was little chance of getting any useful information out of the sheriff, so he said "good day" and walked back to the sail loft.

The afternoon seemed endless as Jem waited for dark. He thought of the long time he had spent searching for his father and of the brief moments they had spent together. He could not believe that his father was dead —not now, not like this. There was only one way he could be certain.

It was two hours after the last, blood-red traces of the summer sun had faded into darkness before Jem and Raif cautiously approached the back door of the funeral parlor on the south end of Postoffice Street. They had watched the front of the place for almost half an hour until old Horace Crumley, Galveston's undertaker, had finally left. Then they ran around to the alley in back.

"We have to hurry," Raif whispered. "He is only going

17

out for supper. With all those bodies to bury tomorrow, he'll be working late tonight."

Jem peeked into the one dirty window, which faced the alley. He saw no sign of movement inside, so he tried to open it quietly. "I think it's been nailed shut," he whispered. "Is there another way in?"

Raif touched the wooden door and it swung open, creaking loudly on its hinges as it moved. "Yes, I am afraid there is — and I think it is a little too easy."

"Why? Old Crumley just forgot to lock it when he went out. I don't see nothin' suspicious about that . . ."

There was a faint rustle of movement somewhere inside and Raif drew back. "What about that?"

"Ain't nothin' but wharf rats. Heck, you know how big some of them get," Jem said and pushed past him. They stepped into the back room of the funeral parlor.

A couple of candles flickered on a table where a body lay covered with a white sheet. Weird, ghostly shadows played among the cobwebs hanging on the walls. Six newly built wooden coffins sat in a neat row on sawhorses. Their tops were open and, even from the doorway, Jem could tell that there was a body in each of them.

Jem's hands were shaking and he was sweating as he tiptoed to the first coffin. The floor creaked with each step. He could hear Raif breathing loudly behind him.

"I think I should wait outside and guard the door," Raif whispered.

Jem did not answer him but stepped up to the first coffin and looked inside. He almost threw up on the floor. The man had been shot directly between the eyes. But Jem forced himself to keep looking, checking each grisly body in turn until he was sure none was his father.

Raif, he noticed, had not left the room but was standing silently beside him as he looked into the last coffin. "*Madre Maria*," he gasped, "that one was almost too big to get in the coffin."

Jem studied the body that was dressed only in a leather vest and canvas pants. He was bald except for a long, black pigtail. On his chest were three small, bluish wounds. "Yeah," Jem said. "And this is the only one who wasn't shot."

"He wasn't?"

Jem pointed at the wounds. "He was stabbed with a real thin blade, three times for sure."

Raif shrugged. "Okay, so we've seen them, and your father is not one of them. Can we leave now?"

"There's still one more," Jem said, pointing to the sheet on the table.

"Well, he can't look any worse than this one," Raif took a deep breath as they moved to the table. Jem pulled back the sheet and Raif gasped. "*Madre Maria*, I have seen that one! I polished his boots just before the shooting started. He tipped me a four-*real*."

"I don't see what killed him."

"He was a strange one, talked like he was English and tipped like he was rich. But he had scars from chains on his wrists, and he wore a gold earring, like the old sailors. See, it's still there."

Jem leaned across the body. His gold locket with the black falcon on it dangled from his neck as he peered at the earring still attached to the man's ear. A sudden terror shot through him.

"C'mon, let's get out of here. We've seen enough." He replaced the sheet, grabbed at Raif's arm, and started pulling him toward the door.

"Hey, what's the hurry? I was just beginning to get used to all this and—"

"C'mon, dang it, let's get out of here," Jem insisted, and together they tiptoed back out into the street. There Jem hesitated for a moment and pointed to a large pile of crates stacked against a warehouse wall.

"We can hide over there," he whispered again and pulled Raif in that direction.

Raif plainly did not understand. "Hide? What do I want to hide for? It is time for this kid to go home and

19

go to sleep, even though he is probably going to have terrible nightmares all night long."

"Just be quiet and hurry."

They slipped behind the crates, and Jem found a place where they could just see the back door to the funeral parlor.

Raif peered out at the dark and empty alley. "What are we doing here?" he asked in a disgusted voice.

"The man with the earring wasn't dead," Jem told him.

"Was not dead? Of course he was dead! Why would anyone who is alive be lying around in the back room of a funeral parlor with a bunch of ugly dead men?"

"He still had his earring."

"What are you talking about?"

"Listen, Raif, the earring was made out of a gold coin. The reason sailors wear them is so if they get killed somewhere, there's always enough money to give 'em a proper buryin'. If that man in there was dead, old Crumley would have taken his earring for payment."

Raif was still thinking about that when the creaking of the funeral parlor door made him look up. A shadowy figure, tall and thin, stepped cautiously into the street and put on his hat.

"See, what'd I tell ya?" Jem whispered.

"I hope you are right, because if you are not, then I am looking at a ghost. And this kid does not like to see ghosts!"

They watched as the figure looked carefully around and then started walking off down the street.

"We should follow him," Jem said, but before he could move, two more dark figures moved into the alley and the boys froze.

"Thompson," one of them growled. "What in the blasted name of Neptune are you doing out here?"

The man turned, his hands already moving toward the pair of Colts in his vest. Then he stopped and seemed to recognize the men in front of him.

"Ah, yes, Mr. Firewhiskers himself. It should be quite obvious why I'm here. I had to find out if those idiots killed Lafitte." He twisted the end of his mustache and grinned. "Besides, one sometimes meets very interesting people in funeral parlors, don't you agree?"

The man called Firewhiskers was even bigger than the pigtailed corpse they had just seen. It was hard to see details in the dark, but he had a huge, reddish beard and a shaggy mop of hair nearly covering his forehead. Both hair and beard were almost as red as his bright silk shirt with large, billowing sleeves. A wide leather belt was barely able to hold a bulging stomach, which almost covered up the two pistols stuck in his belt. His cutlass was supported by another belt across his barrel chest, and two smaller pistols were clipped to the belt.

"You're a lunatic, Thompson," Firewhiskers growled again. "You killed six of our own men today."

"Correction," Thompson noted calmly. "I killed six of *your* men. I would never hire fools who do not follow orders. If you remember correctly, our deal was that, in exchange for my services, I am to have the pleasure of killing Jean Lafitte."

Firewhiskers grumbled behind his beard. "Bilge water. Wouldn't been so bad if you hadn't killed Jongo. Now I had ta go an' hire me another pile of muscles ta do the job on the steam engine." He motioned with one thumb at the other figure who stood just behind him. "This here is Bruno. He's big enough and not much brighter'n Jongo was, and he likes gold. Right, Bruno?"

"Bruno like gold," the other man announced as he lumbered forward. "I bust steamboat for Captain Firewhiskers an' he give me buncha gold. Den Bruno buy big keg 'o rum." He gurgled as he laughed.

"Yes, I should think he will do quite well," Thompson agreed in a disgusted voice. He sniffed the air and then touched a lace handkerchief to his rather long nose. "Come along now, Bruno. Perhaps we can find you a bone to chew on."

22

As the trio walked off down the street, Raif released a breath he had been holding until he was about to burst. "With all the trouble we got, I sure wish *he* had not shown up again."

"Yeah," Jem sighed. "I was sure hopin' we'd seen the last of Bruno. If he ever catches us, we're done for."

4

Jem and Raif watched from their hiding place in the alley as the three men disappeared around the corner. "Something real bad is goin' on an' we gotta find out what it is," Jem said when they were at last out of sight.

"You are right about that," Raif agreed. "Bruno's back in town, and if he finds us, he'll bust our heads."

"Bruno ain't the problem—leastways, he ain't the biggest part of it."

"If he catches us, he is."

"Listen, Raif. Do you know who those other men are?"

Raif shrugged his shoulders. "The fat one called the Englishman 'Thompson.' I thought he called the other one 'Firewhiskers' or something, but I probably did not understand him."

"That's what he called him all right. Mexico Thompson and Johnny Firewhiskers are the two pirates that newspaper story I took to the sheriff was all about. They think those two took the *San Antonio*!"

"Then it does not make any sense to me that they would be here," Raif said, scratching his head.

"Why not? Everybody's lookin' for em way off down in the Caribbean somewhere, when really they're right here in Galveston."

"And Bruno's joined up with them," Raif added. "We should tell the sheriff right away."

"Yeah, but I ain't sure just what it is we're gonna tell him."

"What are you talking about? We are going to tell just what we saw."

"An' what are we going to say we were doing sneakin' into the funeral parlor in the middle of the night to look at dead men?" Jem asked.

"We can just say we heard them talking on the street, and you remembered their names from the newspaper. That way we're not really lying."

Jem shuffled his feet nervously. "I reckon that might work," he admitted solemnly.

"Then come on. We might still catch him at his office." Raif tugged at Jem's arm until he took a couple of slow steps.

"Couldn't we at least wait until tomorrow?" Jem protested. "Maybe by then I can figure out what all this has got to do with my father."

Raif thought for a long moment. "He was trying to get a message to us, and he did say there was some kind of trouble. . . . I don't know, my friend. Do you think he will try to contact you again tonight?"

"Maybe," Jem added hopefully. "If not, we'll go see the sheriff first thing in the morning." With that, the two boys split up, and each headed for home.

All the way back to the sail loft, Jem found himself keeping to the shadows and watching every alleyway and corner. Bruno, he remembered, knew where he lived. It had been in the alley behind the sail loft where Bruno had almost caught him the night their first adventure began over a year ago. He could only hope that Bruno had forgotten all about him and Raif and Talva and their treasure. After all, Bruno was not smart enough to re-member anything very long.

When he got back to the sail loft, he found Uncle Moss sitting in his rocking chair, smoking his crooked pipe and reading a book. Jeffery Reid was writing a letter. Jem poured himself a glass of water from one of the jugs in the kitchen and tried to sound casual when he asked, "Anybody been lookin' for me tonight?"

Uncle Moss lowered his book slowly and looked over his spectacles. "Yep, matter of fact there was. Said they'd come by tomorrow, though, since you was out carousin' 'round town." He huffed and went back to reading his book.

"Well, who was it?" Jem asked anxiously.

"Don't rightly know," Jeffery chimed in without look-ing up. "We never seen her before."

It took a moment for Jem to realize what had been said. "It was a 'her'?"

Uncle Moss was trying his best to keep from laugh-ing. "Pretty one too, and all dressed up real nice. Can't figure why she'd want ta see a ragamuffin like you."

"Aw, come on." Jem was blushing so red that he could feel his ears burning. "I don't know no girls in Galveston. What was her name?"

Uncle Moss shrugged. "Don't recall she ever said. Come to think of it, I don't recall she said where she come from either. Just told us she had to go to the church and she'd speak ta you tomorrow."

Jem was completely confused. Everything was hap-pening at once, and there were too many mysteries to think about. "Well, I don't know nothin' about it," he announced, "and I'm goin' ta bed now."

Uncle Moss watched him start up the stairway to his room. "Lad's been out breakin' hearts already, Jef-fery. Makes a man feel old." Jem could hear them both laughing as he closed the door to his room and hoped they were just playing a joke on him.

"Can't be Talva," Jem muttered. "She ain't pretty . . . leastways, not so you'd notice."

He had never thought of Talva as a regular girl. She was a friend, next to Raif, his best friend, and one who knew the secrets of his past. She had shared their adventures, but Talva loved the forests and bayous. Ever since her mother died, she and her dog, Getana, had lived alone. She fished the bay and wandered wherever she pleased, returning to her house on Lone Oak Bayou to tend her garden. It did not seem likely that she would come to Galveston.

Jem managed to sleep for only a few restless hours that night. Very early the next morning he walked down to the pier where the *Falcon* was docked to check her mooring lines and bail out any water that might have leaked in since yesterday. The sun had risen behind the low outline of Bolivar Island by the time he had finished. He sat for a while on the dock and watched the harbor begin to come to life. Several fishing boats with patched sails of red and tan were working their way out the channel, sailing in short, zigzagging tacks against the south wind. To the west, a little schooner was being hauled alongside McKinnie's Wharf, where a large stack of lumber was waiting to be loaded. And far up in the bay, across Pelican Island and somewhere near HalfMoon Shoal, two faint columns of brown smoke announced the coming of one of the steamboats from Harrisburg.

The morning seemed so peaceful, yet Jem felt certain that something very bad was about to happen — or perhaps it already had happened.

The girl walked so quietly that Jem did not notice her until she was standing right behind him. "Jem?" she said quietly.

He jumped as if he had been shot, then spun around, almost falling in the water as he turned. She wore a white dress with lots of lace and ribbons. Her eyes were as black as her hair, which fell in a cascade of curls across her shoulders. Jem was still staring when she said, "Have you forgotten me so soon?"

Even then, had it not been for the large, yellow dog standing beside her, he might not have been sure. "Talva?" Jem stuttered. "You . . . you look sort of, well . . . different, I guess."

As Talva smiled, Jem thought she looked a lot older, although it had only been a few months since he had last seen her.

"I should hope so," Talva said. "Ben told me that my buckskins would cause people to stare at me in the city. He said I should dress like this." She curtsied and then sat down on the pier beside him.

"I see ya still got Getana," Jem said as he petted the dog beside her.

"Yes," she paused uneasily. "I came to ask if you would let her stay with you for a few days. They will not allow her to go on the steamboat."

Suddenly, things were getting complicated again. "Steamboat?" Jem asked. "You goin' somewhere on a steamboat?"

Talva turned her face away, but there was deep concern in her voice as she said, "The *Powderhorn*, tonight, for Indianola."

"Why ya goin' all the way down there?"

Talva took a deep breath and folded her hands in front of her. "Do you remember when we first met? You were searching for your father then."

"Well, sort of. . . ."

"You were," Talva insisted. "You and Raif may have been following a treasure map and running from Bruno and his friends, but the force that was driving you — making you go on, no matter how bad things got — was your need to know where you came from, your need to find your father."

"I reckon that's the truth, all right. Sometimes now, I think it was easier when I didn't know."

28

"Now it is I who must go in search of my father."

Jem's mouth dropped open. "Ya never talked about it, so I figured ya always knew."

Talva shook her head and her curls bounced lightly on her shoulders. "I fear that my mother did not want me to know everything. Since I last saw you, I have found some things — and I am beginning to believe that your destiny and mine have been woven closely together."

An odd feeling, something like fear but warmer, swept over him. "I don't understand —"

"Neither do I," Talva said and gently took his hand. "But I think it is possible that . . ." She paused and looked directly into his eyes, "I am your sister."

Jem felt as though he had been hit in the head with a jib boom. "But that's impossible!"

"Is it?" Talva answered and held out a gold locket with a black falcon on it, identical to his own.

5

"I found it by accident," Talva said as she handed Jem her own locket. "When we parted last spring on Double Bayou, you knew that I was going to Clear Creek to stay with Old Ben until he recovered from his wound."

"Yeah, and he was gonna build ya a new skiff 'cause yours was sunk when the Mexicans caught ya," Jem added.

"He did, and when it was finished, I sailed it back to my house on Lone Oak Bayou. While I had been away, there had been a lot of rain. Some of the adobe had washed out from the logs on one wall, and my floor was being ruined. I was repairing the damage when I found the locket hidden in the wall."

Jem had removed his own locket, and now he sat turning them both in his hands. "They look just the same," he admitted. "But it still don't make no sense. You met my father. Wouldn't he ah said somethin'?"

Talva shrugged and looked away. "It is a very large puzzle and I do not have all the answers. But I am slowly putting a few of the pieces together."

"That why ya come to Galveston?"

"Ben suggested I look at the church records here to see if there was some mention of my birth. So I went there yesterday and found nothing. But the priest brought some records from the Customs House. They showed that Regina Gray, my mother, came here from Indianola with a child on the 29th of June, in 1837. I would have been five years old then."

"Can you remember anything about it?"

"I remember a ship," Talva said frowning. "And a room somewhere where we lived, perhaps a hotel or boardinghouse, I do not know."

There followed a long silence as Jem and Talva sat together on the pier. "You think you'll find somethin' at Indianola?" Jem asked at last.

"It seems to be the next step. I have come too far to turn back now."

Sheriff Smythe reread the wanted poster he had just had printed, then looked doubtfully over his spectacles at the two boys who stood before him. "And you say you heard this here Mexico Thompson fellow talking to this other man and calling him 'Firewhiskers' right here in Galveston last night?"

"Yes, sir," Jem gulped and twitched nervously under the sheriff's stern stare.

"It is just like we told you," Raif chimed in. "We were walking home last night and we saw them. They looked kind of mean, so we hid behind some big boxes and then we heard them talking."

"In the alley behind the funeral parlor?" the sheriff added suspiciously and scratched his chin. "Mr. Crumley told me just this morning that he thinks somebody was sneaking around inside his place last night while he was out having his supper. Now, that wouldn't have been you boys, would it?"

Jem gulped again but before he could answer, Raif spoke up. "Us? Why would we be sneaking around in some place full of dead people? I do not like dead people

31

—they are all spooky-looking and they give me these little goose bumps. See? I am getting them now just thinking about them—"

"All right," the sheriff broke in. "I'll check into it as soon as I get some time."

"Thank you very much, sheriff," Raif said as he pulled Jem by the collar toward the door. "Come on my friend, we have to go now."

"I told ya he wouldn't believe us," Jem sighed as they walked down the street. "An' now he figures *we* were sneakin' around the funeral parlor."

"Well, you know how grown-up people are; sometimes they are not too good at getting things right," Raif concluded. "Which means that we will have to find out what is going on all by ourselves."

Jem was not impressed with Raif's logic. "An' how we supposed ta do that?" he asked.

Raif stopped at the corner of Postoffice Street and the Strand. "Well, my friend, do not forget that I control the shoeshine business in all of Galveston."

"Yeah, so what?"

"So I will give a description of the men we saw to all four of my shoeshine boys, and if they see one of them, they will come and tell me. Of course, I will have to move them around some and it will be bad for business, but I will do it.

"Let me see, José is at Alphonse's Boarding House. I will move him down to the Morgan Line Wharf. And Joey Brighton can cover McKinnie's Wharf. That still leaves me here and Juan Morales to work the east end of the Strand." Raif nodded his head, satisfied that he had the city covered. He hooked his thumbs behind his suspenders and leaned against the porch of the Tremont. "If anyone is moving around, one of my men will spot them for sure."

Jem thought for a moment and decided it sounded like a good plan, even if Raif had been the one to come up with it. "Okay, I'll check around the wharves too.

And remember: I'll meet you tonight when the *Powder-horn* sails. We'll see Talva off."

"I'll be there," Raif assured him and then added, "Watch out for Bruno."

Talva awoke slowly. The shadows on the wall of her room at Alphonse's Boarding House told her that she had slept away most of the hot afternoon. Her head hurt as she sat up and realized that she had gone to sleep with her locket clutched tightly in her hand. She stared across the tiny room to where Getana was lying beside her one small traveling case.

"It is time," she said as she placed the locket around her neck and concealed it beneath the lace of her dress. Getana followed her silently to the door and down the stairs. They passed quietly through the common room and onto a porch that faced the street.

It was there that Talva ran straight into Mexico Thompson, who was carrying a large case and two carpet-bags. Before it was over, she found herself sitting flat on the wooden planks of the porch.

"I say, lass, are you hurt?" Thompson asked as he offered her his hand.

"I—I do not think so," Talva answered uncertainly as she was helped to her feet and dusted off her dress.

"Terribly sorry. That was most clumsy of me, by George, it was."

Talva looked up into his tan face and sparkling blue eyes. She noticed the long scar on his right cheek and the earring in his left ear. "It was my fault as well," she admitted. "I—I am not exactly at home here."

"Quite so," Thompson answered. "Your speech hardly marks you as a native of this godforsaken island."

"Neither does yours," Talva said.

"Well-said," he laughed. "But please, pardon my manners and allow me to introduce myself. I am Sir Thomas Jones, formerly of His Majesty's Navy and currently a dealer in ship's stores, cordage, hardware, and the like."

33

"I am called 'Talva,' and this is Getana," she answered.

Thompson went suddenly silent. A faraway look flashed across his face and vanished as quickly as it had come. "And might I inquire as to where your home is?" he pried. "I'm sort of a student of accents, you might say. Yours is quite lovely, but I cannot place it."

Talva stared at him for a moment. Ben had warned her not to talk to strangers in Galveston. "My home is north, on Lone Oak Bayou. But my mother was born someplace far away. She called it 'Salem'."

Thompson frowned for a second and then nodded. "Salem, in the far-off state of Massachusetts? Well, that explains it." He paused and then pointed to a carriage waiting in the street. "I've engaged a rig to transport my baggage and myself to the Morgan Line Wharf. I see that you are leaving also. Might I offer you and your mother a lift somewhere?"

"I am traveling alone," Talva assured him bluntly, "on the *Powderhorn*."

At this, the stranger seemed stunned. Talva noticed the sparkle vanish from his eyes and he looked away. "But, if Getana may come also, I would be happy to ride in your carriage," Talva said suddenly and was surprised at herself for accepting.

"Wouldn't have it any other way," Thompson announced as he held open the carriage door. "We should be off—I believe our ship sails within the hour."

"You are sailing on the *Powderhorn* also?" Talva asked when she stepped in.

"I've a bit of business in—in Indianola." Getana bounced into the seat beside Talva and sat quietly eying the stranger as the carriage drove off. "A fine animal you have there. Excellent protection, I'm sure." He extended his hand cautiously and Getana ignored it.

"She is not sure of you yet," Talva said, petting the dog's neck. "It is as if she is seeing two people."

"A wise animal."

They rode in silence through the streets of Galveston until the carriage rattled to a stop beside the steamboat *Powderhorn*. "Thank you for the lift. I had never ridden in a carriage before," Talva said as she stepped out onto the dock.

Jem and Raif had just finished watching three deputy sheriffs load fifteen cases of Colt revolvers aboard the *Powderhorn*. They were sitting on a couple of pilings when they saw the carriage drive up and Talva get out. "Hey, that is pretty fancy," Raif exclaimed as she approached them. "How did you get a ride in a rig like that?"

"That nice man gave me a lift," Talva said, pointing to the carriage, but Thompson was now hidden from view as he supervised the unloading of his baggage. "Well, I don't see him right now." She set down her bag and hugged Getana's neck. "Stay here with Jem and Raif, and keep them out of trouble. I will be back in a few days."

Raif held onto Getana as Jem and Talva walked slowly toward the *Powderhorn*'s gangplank. "Reckon I oughta be goin' with ya," Jem said and scuffed his feet.

"There is nothing you could do there. And, whatever I learn in Indianola, you will be the only one I will ever tell." Talva touched his hand for a moment and then walked away up the gangplank.

Jem had strolled back to where Raif was waiting before he turned to look at the *Powderhorn*. Three blasts echoed from her whistle, and crewmen began clearing away the lines that held her to the dock. From inside the open engine room door, someone was singing as he stoked wood into one of the boilers:

> *Fifteen men on da dead man's chest,*
> *Yo ho ho und da bottle of rum . . .*

Both boys froze in their tracks and looked at each other. "Bruno?" they said at the same time.

"Yes, and he's on the *Powderhorn* with Talva!"

Raif was pointing to the *Powderhorn*'s upper deck, where a few passengers were leaning against the rail. "*Madre Maria*, that is not the worst of it. Look up there! Is that not Mexico Thompson?"

Jem saw Talva standing beside Thompson. For a moment Jem felt completely helpless. The *Powderhorn* had taken in her dock lines and her huge paddlewheels were splashing up water as they started to turn her away from the dock. As the bow swung away, the stern moved closer to the dock.

"I gotta get aboard!" he said excitedly.

"You cannot do that. If you jump, you'll get killed by the paddlewheels! Besides, you don't have a ticket!"

Jem pointed to a small space between the cotton bales piled on the *Powderhorn*'s afterdeck. "I can jump for it when the stern gets a little closer," Jem said as he backed up for a running start.

"You are crazy. Don't do that!" Raif was pleading as Jem started to run. The *Powderhorn*'s whistle screamed again as her paddlewheels changed direction and the stern started to move away from the dock. The space between the cotton bales seemed very small and very far away as Jem ran with all his might. He jumped from the dock and, for a moment, felt weightless and spinning as dark water churned below him.

6

Jem fell against the cotton bales and landed on his head on the *Powderhorn*'s stern. For a moment everything seemed to be spinning. In the fading twilight, he could feel the ship's roll and hear her steam engine throbbing beneath the deck. Getana was barking in his ear, and someone was calling for help as he staggered to his feet and looked around.

"Raif?" he called and realized that the voice was coming from over the ship's side. He staggered to the rail and there was Raif, clinging by his fingertips to the *Powderhorn*'s stern and kicking his feet wildly.

"Hold on!" Jem grabbed Raif's collar to pull him aboard. "Ya gotta help me, dang it all!" he grunted.

"I am trying, I am trying!" Raif wailed and kicked more. They made little progress until Getana put her teeth on the sleeve of Raif's shirt and pulled also. Slowly, inch by inch, they dragged him onto the deck.

"Why'd you try to jump?" Jem asked.

Raif panted and sat up on one elbow. "You can be sure that it was not my idea! Getana is the one who decided she was going with you. I was just holding on, trying to stop her."

Jem looked out over the stern. The last trace of twilight was a deep purple glow behind the Galveston skyline. "I don't think anybody saw us," he said, surprised after all the noise they had made. The dock was a hundred yards away and marked now by only a line of dim, yellow lanterns. The *Powderhorn* picked up speed with every turn of her paddlewheels.

They heard voices, just on the other side of the cotton bales, as several crewmen began tying down the deck cargo. The steamboat rounded Snake Point and headed out into the Gulf.

"We are going to be in a lot of trouble when they find us. I heard they throw stowaways overboard sometimes," Raif said as he and Jem pressed themselves closely against the bales.

"Yep, so we better be real careful that we don't get found."

Both passengers and crewmen continued to pass close by them for what seemed like several hours. By the time things quieted down, the *Powderhorn* was far out into the Gulf of Mexico. The lights of Galveston were only a faint glow behind them.

Carefully, they peeked out from their hiding place. Getana was whining beside them as Raif whispered, "It is going to be hard enough just to keep her quiet and out of sight, much less ourselves."

Jem scratched his head. "You think she'll stay here if we tell her to?"

"Maybe, if we are not gone too long," Raif answered.

"I figure if we could get into the engine room, maybe we can find out what Bruno's up to."

Raif pointed his finger in Getana's face and said, "Stay! We will come back very soon." To their surprise, the dog lay down quietly. Raif shrugged and followed Jem as he climbed over the cotton bales and started forward.

Before the boys had gone more than a few yards, two crewmen appeared around the corner and the boys dove into the shadows. They passed near enough that Jem could have touched them.

"That was close," Raif whispered, taking a deep breath as again they started making their way along the deck.

The engine room was located almost amidship. Low doors were left open on both sides to give some relief to the engineer and fireman who had to work inside.

As Jem approached the open doorway, the noise from inside grew steadily louder. The steam engine pounded with an ear-splitting rhythm. A blast of heat hit Jem's face as he peeked inside. Everywhere were steam pipes, gauges, and valves. In the middle of the jungle of machinery were two black iron boilers. Each one looked as big as a house. Behind them, in the orange glow of their fireboxes, was Bruno, throwing in pieces of wood and stoking the fires. He had removed his shirt and his huge body was shiny with sweat — and bigger than they remembered.

Raif tapped Jem's shoulder just as another figure appeared suddenly on deck and headed toward him. "Quick, Jem, we need a place to hide!"

Just behind the boilers were two large fuel bunkers, bins for storing firewood. They looked like the only chance. Jem pointed to them and Raif nodded. They still had to wait another moment until Bruno's back was turned before darting into the engine room.

They almost made it. The bunkers were only a few feet away when Bruno suddenly turned and looked straight at them.

"Duh, hi dere." Bruno smiled and showed several missing teeth. "What you little guys do down here?"

"I — I think we are lost," Raif said. "We were looking for the kitchen."

Bruno squinted his little eyes and his stupid smile vanished. "Hey! I know youse guys. You hit Bruno wit rock, you sick big dog on Bruno, den you get all dat treasure and Bruno get dog bite." With that, Bruno picked up a length of firewood, about as long as Jem was tall. "Bruno bust heads," he growled, but Jem and Raif were already running.

They ducked beneath some steam pipes and scurried up one of the narrow iron catwalks which ran down the side of each boiler.

"You no hide from Bruno dis time!" the huge man said as he charged after them.

Besides the flickering glow from the fireboxes, there were only a few small lanterns hung here and there to light the engine room. This was definitely to the boys' advantage. The only problem was that somewhere near the forward end of the starboard boiler, Jem went one way and Raif went another.

When Jem stopped to look back, he could hear Bruno's stick banging against the machinery. He ducked under the catwalk and waited.

Bruno's big feet clumped along the catwalk above him. "Bruno gonna find you, Bruno gonna find you," he was saying over and over.

As Jem held his breath and watched from hiding, he suddenly saw Mexico Thompson in front of Bruno. "What the devil are you doing, man?"

Bruno stopped banging his stick on the engine. "Bruno hunt little people."

"Oh, really," Thompson said in a bored voice and raised one eyebrow.

"Bruno chase 'em. Dey got treasure."

Thompson, of course, had no idea what he was talking about. "By George," he said to no one in particular, "the bloke's gone batty. I do believe he's hunting leprechauns."

Bruno would have kept banging on things, but Thompson stopped him. "You do know what you are supposed to do?"

Bruno nodded his big head several times. "Oh sure, Bruno know." He looked around at the huge steam engine with its countless rods and levers and pistons. "Duh, dat one, right dere."

"Yes, quite right," Thompson nodded, looking at the main steam reverse valves. "Put a bar behind it and pull as hard as you can. It will break and the engine will stop. But we'll be able to fix it in a matter of minutes. Any questions?"

Bruno shook his head again and again. "Bruno bust da boat, Bruno bust da boat."

"But not until I tell you," Thompson finished and looked at his watch. "Now, if you will excuse me, I am dining with a most interesting young lady."

He pushed past Bruno, who turned to watch him go. "Dat man talk funny," he said after Thompson had left.

Jem stayed hidden until Bruno had walked back to the firebox doors. Then he looked around for Raif. "Reckon he must have snuck out," Jem thought and quietly worked his way back to the engine room door. He peeked out and saw the deck deserted.

Jem started making his way carefully back to the stern, figuring that Raif would return to where they had left Getana. He passed the doorways to several darkened cabins on the way. As he passed the last one, he heard a creaking noise behind him and turned just in time to see a dark figure reach for him. He swung a wild right, which connected, and a left hook, which missed, before a hand went over his mouth and pulled him into the dark cabin.

The *Powderhorn*'s main salon was the fanciest dining room that Talva had ever seen. A dozen polished brass lamps swung in lazy circles overhead. Drapes of crushed red velvet bordered the large windows, which now looked out over a moonlit sea. There were columns of varnished wood supporting the deck above. And on each table was a brass lamp and a small vase with fresh flowers.

41

Talva sat across from Mexico Thompson and sipped her tea from a crystal glass. She stared deeply into his eyes, trying to see inside this tall, thin man with the English accent. But everything about him confused her, and Talva was a girl who was not easily confused.

Several times, she tried to clear her mind and find his aura, that magical haze around the head which her mother had once taught her to see. "Only dead people have no aura," her mother had said. But this man's was so faded that she could not find it. Or perhaps, she thought, the unfamiliar surroundings made it impossible to concentrate properly.

His lies, which normally would have infuriated her, did not seem important tonight. She was certain that his name was not Sir Thomas Jones and that he was not a salesman as he claimed to be. But most of the rest of what he said seemed to be true, and she sensed that the lies he told were hurting him as much as they were her.

His eyes sparkled with fond memories when he told of sea battles during the War of 1812. "I was a shave-tail lieutenant then," he laughed. "Third officer on the old frigate *Indomitable*. The admirals sent us chasing French privateers off Grand Terre. Nasty fellows they were, fast little schooners and brigantines that attacked you at night and then slipped back up into the swamps. But enough of me," he said finally. "Tell me, what sends you traveling alone to Indianola? I should think your mother would be worried sick about you."

Talva felt suddenly uncomfortable. "My mother has been dead for three years." She hesitated, but when Thompson said nothing, she continued reluctantly. "I believe there may be some records of my birth at Indianola."

"Really?" Thompson paused and then said, "Interesting, quite interesting." There was a faraway look in his eyes as he added, "And might I be so bold as to inquire about your father?"

Talva's eyes dropped to the white lace tablecloth in front of her. "My mother told me that he died at sea." She almost added that her mother had not always told her the truth, but she stopped herself in time.

"I see," Thompson said quietly. "Your name," he added after an awkward pause. "It means 'Spring' I believe. Did your mother give you that name?"

Talva's fork rattled loudly against her plate. "How would you know—" she started, but he raised his hand.

"I knew a woman once in New Orleans. She was . . . she was a . . ."

"A witch?" There was a note of growing anger in Talva's voice.

Thompson smiled and shook his head. "Hardly, although some called her so. She was — sensitive. She could feel things, know things sometimes before they happened. She could tell when a storm was brewing out in the Gulf sometimes days before it arrived." His eyes drifted off as if he were in deep thought. "She would talk to the plants in the garden and make them grow. Animals and birds seemed to just pop in from everywhere whenever they were sick or injured. Somehow, she could always make them well again."

"And you loved her very much."

Thompson blinked his eyes twice and took another sip of tea. "Yes," he said, clearing his throat. "I suppose I did."

Thompson removed a gold watch from his vest pocket. "Dear me, it's quite late and I've some business that must be attended to." He replaced the watch hurriedly and dabbed at his mouth with a napkin as he rose. "Do excuse me. It's been a most enjoyable evening."

Talva watched him step out on deck and hurry off somewhere toward the ship's stern. A strange chill rushed through her, and she trembled as she tried to finish her dessert.

7

It was completely dark inside the cabin as Jem struggled with his captor. He bit down hard on the hand which was over his mouth and was rewarded with a quiet curse behind him.

"Jeremiah!" a voice whispered loudly in the darkness.

Jem stopped struggling, and the strong hands released him. "Father!" he blurted out without thinking.

"Yes, yes, but be very quiet."

Jem lowered his voice to a whisper. "What are you doing here?"

"The same thing as you, I suspect, trying to find out what Monsieur Thompson is up to." A flint sparked and one of the cabin's whale oil lamps was lighted. In a moment, Jem stood facing his father.

Lafitte still wore the tattered blue seaman's coat and baggy trousers Raif had described, and he still carried a cane. He smiled behind a week-old beard. "It is good to see you, my son."

Jem returned the smile as he relaxed a little. "Glad

44

ta see you too. Thought for a while you was a goner after all that shootin' at the Tremont."

Lafitte nodded. "That was closer than I prefer. And also very strange. I received some unexpected help from someone I had long ago thought dead."

"Mexico Thompson?" Jem asked.

His father nodded. "How do you know of him?"

"Well, first, I seen a paper from New Orleans. Then me an' Raif heard him talkin' to a big, mean-lookin' guy with a red beard called 'Johnny Firewhiskers'." Jem paused and looked away. "Paper said they used ta sail with you."

"Johnny Firewhiskers did. I even sold him a ship named *Le Brave* and secured his Letters of Marque — one of my many mistakes." Lafitte scratched his chin. "As for Mexico Thompson, we met quite differently. I took an English frigate during the War of 1812. Her captain was killed after they had struck their colors. Thompson was the first officer. He demanded satisfaction — so we fought a duel and he was badly wounded. Some years later, we met again on the Yucatan. Much of the world thinks he killed me there."

"You give him that scar on his face?" Jem asked.

Lafitte laughed bitterly. "Mexico Thompson has many scars. Some can be seen, others are deep inside and will never heal. But that is a long story."

"I heard him talking to Bruno in the engine room. He was tellin' him how to break the engine."

"Then it is as I suspected. Thompson and Firewhiskers are planning to take this ship and to steal the shipment of Colt revolvers. I would hate to see those guns end up in their hands. But they are up to something much worse than that."

"What could be worse than that?"

"For some time now, Firewhiskers has been waiting for the Texas Navy to be disbanded. The American Navy is busy hunting him in the Caribbean, so he has moved his base to a secret location, somewhere along the Texas coast, where he will attack every ship which passes."

"And with no navy patrollin' and all those new Colt revolvers, there won't be nothin' that can beat him!" Jem realized. "How we gonna stop 'em?"

Lafitte scratched at his chin. "An excellent question. Unfortunately, I do not have an answer for it. I am sure that you and I alone cannot keep them from taking this ship."

"But what else can we do?"

"My own ship should not be too far away. Now, on the *Powderhorn*'s stern is a small rowboat. I hid a few things aboard it earlier. If we can get to it and launch it, we may be able to reach her and then we can deal with Monsieur Firewhiskers."

"I can't leave," Jem said anxiously. "Raif and Talva are aboard somewhere."

Lafitte shook his head as he moved toward the door. "Firewhiskers has at least one well-armed ship out there somewhere and the largest crew of cutthroats I have ever seen. If we are still aboard the *Powderhorn* when he attacks, we will be no help to anyone."

Jem was silent as they slipped out of the cabin. A few scattered clouds had covered the moon, and a stiff breeze was blowing up from the south. They made their way back toward the stern, and there, among the deck cargo of cotton bales, was a small skiff with two oars. Lafitte quickly untied the lines that secured it.

"All right, now help me push it into the water," Lafitte said.

"I can't go!" Jem said suddenly.

Lafitte stopped pushing on the boat. He looked at Jem for a long moment and then said, "Try to find your friends. I will wait as long as possible."

"Okay! I'll find 'em!" Jem blurted out and hurried forward. He got only a few feet before running straight into someone. The collision knocked him down, and he was scrambling to his feet before he realized that he had hit Mexico Thompson. "Look out, Father!" he yelled as he was shoved back toward the stern and tripped again.

The tall man in the tan suit towered above him. A Colt revolver was in his left hand and a gold-handled sword was in his right. His eyes moved from Jem to his father and back again. "Yes, of course," Thompson was saying. "Should have realized it when I saw that locket last night. You're Lafitte's own son. It's obvious by the look of you."

Lafitte rose slowly from beside the rowboat. The cane was still in his hand. "Ah, good evening, Monsieur Thompson. Again we meet. It has been a long time since that day on the Yucatan."

"Much too long," Thompson answered bitterly. "I could have killed you at the Tremont."

"I suspect you missed an excellent opportunity —one which I shall try not to give you again," Lafitte answered evenly. He moved away from the boat.

"I believe you already have," Thompson said in an unpleasant tone as he took a step toward Lafitte.

The cane flashed in Lafitte's hand and separated just below the handle, exposing a long, thin blade.

"Ah, a sword cane. Yes, of course," Thompson commented as he holstered his pistol but kept the sword ready in front of him. "I wondered how you could have killed Jongo so quickly. Actually, at first I wasn't sure which of us had killed him."

With that, Thompson lunged and Lafitte deftly parried the blow, took a step backward, and thrust high, catching a few threads of Thompson's coat. The ring of steel against steel was lost in the rumble of *Powderhorn*'s steam engine and the whine of the sea wind.

Jem found himself unable to move until his father yelled to him, "Find your friends, quickly!" Jem scrambled to his feet and ran toward the bow of the ship. He took the first stairway he came to and ran up to the cabin deck. He was about where he thought Talva's cabin should be when he saw Raif running as fast as he could toward him.

"Raif, over here!" he called. His friend came puffing up to a stop. "We gotta find Talva and get off this ship real fast. My father's got a skiff on the stern!"

"Your father, he is —?"

"Ain't got time for explainin' now. You seen Talva?"

"Yes," Raif panted. "She was in the dining room, that was just before the cook and two of the waiters saw me. They have been chasing me ever since." Even as Raif spoke, the ship's cook, still in his white apron and tall hat, came around the corner with a meat cleaver in his hand. Not far behind him were two white-coated waiters from the dining room.

"Look, there's another one," the cook yelled. "He's not one of the passengers either. Get 'em!"

Jem was already running the other way when they heard the lookout's voice call from the hurricane deck above them. "Sail ho! Close off the starboard bow and showing no lights! She looks like a derelict."

"Could it already be starting?" Jem thought. At the sound of the lookout's call, the waiters and cook suddenly lost interest in chasing stowaways and stopped to look at the distant ship.

"*Madre Maria,*" Raif gasped and pointed seaward. "It looks like a ghost."

At that moment, the moon slipped from behind a cloud and bathed the sea in a pale, eerie light. The ship was a schooner, drifting aimlessly with one of her jibs set and the other apparently torn and streaming out over her bow. A topsail was also set, but one corner had come loose and it slapped out an uneven rhythm as the ship rose and fell with the sea.

The *Powderhorn* had slowed down and turned toward the darkened ship. From where they stood on the cabin deck, Jem and Raif could see the *Powderhorn*'s pilot house on the hurricane deck above them. As they drew alongside, they saw one of the ship's officers step out with a brass speaking trumpet to hail the silent ship.

"Hello the schooner!" he called. "Do you need help?" He was answered only by the distant cry of sea gulls and the restless slapping of waves against the hull.

"Ease her in close. We'll put a man aboard her," the captain called, and *Powderhorn*'s paddlewheels turned slowly forward.

"I know that ship!" Jem said, suddenly realizing that he had helped cut the jib which now flapped in the wind before him. "She's the *San Antonio*!" he gasped and then yelled as loud as he could toward the wheelhouse. "It's a trap, get away from her, she's a pirate!"

The captain stared down at Jem. For a long moment, he looked confused as the distance between the two ships narrowed to only a few yards. Then suddenly he turned and ordered, "Full reverse! Back us off!"

For a second, the *Powderhorn*'s paddlewheels reversed, but then there was a loud clanging noise below decks. The engine stopped dead, and the two ships drifted together with a solid thud which rattled the schooner's rigging and shook the *Powderhorn*'s deck.

From the engine room below, they heard a familiar voice. "Bruno bust da boat!"

For one last chilling moment, there was silence. Then laughter, wicked and evil, rose from the dark schooner. A dim orange glow appeared by her wheel as a huge, bearded figure rose, holding a lighted match in one hand. Still laughing, he touched the match to his beard, and it caught fire, glowing and smoldering in a dozen different spots. "Boarders away!" he shrieked, waving a cutlass above his head. Jem suddenly realized why he was called "Johnny Firewhiskers."

A blood-curdling battle cry rose from the schooner and drowned out the sounds of wind and sea. Dozens of dark figures, armed with cutlasses and pistols, swarmed over the schooner's side and onto the *Powderhorn*. The captain fell in a hail of musket balls that blasted out the pilot house windows. Women were screaming and men were yelling. Smoke from the musket fire swept up around the cabin deck, turning the whole scene into a nightmare of terror.

Jem and Raif were running for the main salon where Talva had last been seen. As they reached the stairway down to the main deck, they were met by a pirate charging up the stairs and swinging his cutlass in their direction. Almost running over each other, the two boys retreated back up to the cabin deck and ran forward, dodging the cook who was now struggling with no less than three of the pirates.

By the time they had reached the next set of stairs, which led down to the ship's bow, most of the fighting was over. Several pirates were inside the pilot house and others were herding passengers into the main salon.

"We're too danged late!" Jem panted, trying to catch his breath.

"No, look there!" Raif cried out, pointing to the hurricane deck above them. Cornered against the forward railing was Talva. Getana was by her side, snarling and growling as three pirates moved cautiously toward her.

"Shoot the dog," one of them hissed. "The girl might bring a fair price in Mexico."

Before anything else could happen, Mexico Thompson suddenly appeared behind them. "Leave her alone," he said in a cold voice.

"Now just who in the bloody—" one of the pirates started to say as he swung a cutlass in Thompson's direction. His sentence went unfinished as Thompson clubbed him with the barrel of one of his revolvers.

"Talva," Thompson called, "don't be afraid, you are under my protection now."

Talva backed closer to the rail. "You are one of them," she snarled. "If you are my only choice, then I choose to die in the sea."

Thompson took a step toward her. His voice sounded desperate. "No wait, I have to know. Are you—?"

"Do not come near me! I was a prisoner once, and I shall never be one again!" Talva screamed at him. There

were tears on her cheeks and her whole body trembled as she pointed a finger at his face. Her eyes went pale and seemed to glow with a green fire. Jem thought he saw tiny blue sparks dancing on her fingertip. "Stay away!" she warned again.

Thompson stopped in his tracks. One of his pistols clattered on the deck at his feet. "My God," he gasped, "you *do* belong to her!" He staggered a couple of steps backward. "No!" he cried out as Talva climbed onto the railing. "Don't jump!" Again, he started forward, but it was too late.

For a moment, Talva turned her eyes toward Jem and Raif, as if to say goodbye. Then she dove from the rail, her arms spread and her back arched in a graceful swan dive, into the dark waters below.

"Talva!" Jem cried out with all his might. For a long moment, he could not move. He could not make himself believe that she had really jumped. He wanted to cry, but no tears would come. Instead, he felt an anger building inside him, destroying all other feelings. The whole, horrible scene reflected through a fog of crimson rage as he climbed the stairs to the hurricane deck. Getana was running back and forth along the rail, constantly barking. Then she too bounded over the rail and vanished into the dark, swirling waters far below.

Jem was only vaguely aware of Raif tugging at his arm as he ran at Thompson and began to hit him. His blows seemed to have no effect. Thompson stood with his hands at his sides, staring dumbly over the railing as Jem hit him again and again.

"You killed her, you killed her!" Jem cried over and over until at last someone knocked him to the deck.

Raif was talking to him, telling him to be quiet and not fight anymore as he tried to get up. Firewhiskers was standing over him. His ugly, hairy face was surrounded by wisps of stinking, gray smoke. A dripping towel was in his hand, and he was putting out the last smoldering sparks in his beard.

"A good trick, eh, lad?" Firewhiskers said, pointing at his smoking beard. "Scares the living daylights outta reasonable folk, it does, especially if they's got religion. Makes 'em think the devil hisself has come for their blasted souls." From his beard he removed what looked like a short piece of rope and held it in front of Jem's nose. "Slow match, same's we use for the cannons, that's the trick of it. Ya gotta dip 'em in saltpeter and limewater though, elseways ya burns yerself bald as a sea gull egg."

Firewhiskers leaned over until his face was inches away from Jem's nose. He smelled like a mixture of bilge water and rotten fish. "Blackbeard hisself used ta light his beard like this over a hundred years ago. Some says I looks a bit like 'im." With that, he raised back up and roared with laughter. The rest of his pirate crew, except for Mexico Thompson, joined in.

As the laughter died away, Firewhiskers turned to Thompson, who was still staring out at the dark sea. He patted two Colt revolvers, now in his own belt. "Well, Thompson, we took 'em. Your plan worked. Now we've got two hundred of these and the fastest steamship on the coast. There's been many an empire built on less. Soon's we get her stripped out and pierced for cannon, we'll have the finest fightin' ship what ever flew the Jolly Roger."

Thompson looked up as if trying to snap out of his daze. "Did you find Lafitte yet?"

"What are ye babblin' about?" Firewhiskers growled.

"He was aboard, dressed as a seaman. When the attack started, I lost him."

Firewhiskers turned to his crew. "Search every inch of this ship," he ordered in a nervous voice. "Find him or I'll hang ya all from the yardarms! While you're at it, dump the deck cargo and some of that fancy furniture outta the salon. We'll make 'em think she blew a boiler, went down with all hands."

As most of the crew hurried off, Firewhiskers gave Thompson a crooked stare. "Matey, ya look like ya seen a ghost."

Thompson took one more look back out at the sea. "Perhaps I have," he answered quietly. "Perhaps I have."

Firewhiskers turned back to Jem and Raif. "Well now, what shall I do with the two of you?" He scratched at his beard and then answered his own question. "Put you with the rest of the passengers, I suppose. Maybe there's somebody be willing ta pay ta get ya back. And if not, well now, that would be so much the worse for you."

At that moment, Bruno came lumbering up onto the hurricane deck and saw the two boys. "Hey dere, dat's dose little guys. Bruno want bust dere heads. Can Bruno bust dere heads now? Huh, Captain Firewhiskers, can Bruno, huh, huh?"

Firewhiskers shrugged his shoulders and his belly shook. "Why not? They're yours Bruno. I make you a present of them."

Bruno was gurgling with laughter as he grabbed both boys by their collars and lifted them off the deck. "Maybe Bruno don't bust your heads," he mumbled. "Maybe Bruno feed you to sharks. Sharks like tender little nippers."

"Come on now, Bruno," Raif was pleading. "You wouldn't have any fun doing that."

Bruno thought about that for a moment and then said, "Bruno have fun, Bruno have lots of fun!" With a boy still hanging in each arm, he waddled to the rail and held them over the side. "Here sharks, here sharky, sharky. Come and get your dinner now."

From his dangling position, almost three stories high, Jem saw the *Powderhorn*'s paddlewheel begin to turn. He felt sick and tried not to look down.

Firewhiskers stood watching them from the deck. As Bruno jerked him up and down, still laughing and calling the sharks, Jem saw Firewhiskers take a musket away from one of his men and start toward them.

"Look out, Bruno, behind you!" Raif yelled, but Bruno just kept laughing and shaking the two boys.

"Dat old trick," Bruno mumbled again as Firewhiskers gripped the musket by its barrel and raised it over his head. "What you think, Bruno stupid? Fall for old trick like dat?"

"It ain't no trick, ya dumb ox, he's gonna—" Jem's sentence was never finished. The musket butt slammed into Bruno's head with a hollow crack.

"Dat hurt," he said, and then his eyes rolled back in his head and he fell forward over the rail, releasing the boys as he fell.

Jem heard air whistle past his ears and saw the dark water rushing up at him. He was falling head first, he realized just before he hit. The water was harder than he imagined it would be. The impact tried to push the air out of his lungs as his head went under, and he fought to hold his breath. The ocean pulled him down, down —deeper, he thought, than he had ever been before. He wondered what dying was going to be like.

9

As Jem's head broke water, the first thing he saw was the *Powderhorn*'s paddlewheel, its huge blades threatening to crush him as they turned. White water, bright and unreal in the moonlight, churned all around him, and the steam engine drummed in his ears. Jem gulped in air and swam with all his might. He felt the suction from the paddlewheel, spinning him around and pulling him closer to the deadly blades. A wave broke over him, blinding him and filling his mouth with salt water. He was no longer sure which way he was swimming.

The paddlewheel blades crashed in the water beside him. For an instant, one touched him, ripped at his shirt, and then flung him away. His head grazed once against the ship's hull. Then he was forced away and wallowed in the swirling water of her wake.

There was a stinging pain in Jem's shoulder as he treaded water and watched the ship's lights grow smaller as she steamed away from him. The pirate schooner had hoisted sail and was also moving away.

"Gotta take it easy," Jem told himself as he fought to stay afloat. His shoes were dragging him down, so he kicked them off and let them sink beneath him. He lay back then, with his face just above the water, and found that he had to work less to stay afloat in that position. "Jes' like swimmin' backstroke," he said, wondering how much longer it would be before he drowned.

A million stars hung above him like sparkling diamonds. He could never remember there being so many. It was hard to find the Big Dipper. He had to turn himself several times to pick it out among so many other stars. But it was there, pointing to the North Star, just like always. "Reckon land would be that way," he thought. He had no idea how far offshore *Powderhorn* had been when the attack came.

"Maybe I oughta swim north until I either touch land or drown," he considered as he rose and fell with the constant rocking of the sea. "Might be better'n jes' floatin' here."

On the crest of the next wave, he looked around and tried to get his bearings. He had turned until he was again facing the North Star and was about to start swimming when he thought he saw a dark shape bobbing just past the next wave. Jem blinked the salt out of his eyes and looked again as another wave lifted him. Shadows danced along each wave, playing tricks in the darkness. For a moment he thought he was imagining it, and then, there it was again.

Still uncertain exactly what was floating in front of him, Jem swam for it. His hand reached out, missed it on the first try, and then grabbed a piece of wet rope. "A cotton bale," he said aloud as he pulled himself partly up, out of the water. He coughed out a mouthful of sea water and climbed a little higher. "I remember now. Firewhiskers told 'em ta dump the deck cargo, ta make it look like she sunk."

"Yes, I am very glad that he did," a familiar voice answered from the other side of the cotton bale.

"Raif?" Jem almost screamed. "Is that you?"

"Yes, of course it is me. And just like always, it was a big mistake to go anywhere with you. You always get me in trouble, and so far this is the worst! I am even too tired to pull myself out of the water."

With a bit of renewed strength, Jem crawled to the edge of the cotton bale and helped Raif pull himself up beside him. Then they both dropped, exhausted.

"Do you think Talva might have made it?" Raif asked. It sounded as if he had been crying.

"Might have," Jem answered, trying to sound hopeful. "She's a good swimmer, and she's pretty smart, for a girl."

For a long time neither of them spoke. Jem soon found that it was impossible to rest very much while clinging to a water-soaked cotton bale. "This is about as comfortable as tryin' ta lay down on a horse's back while it's runnin'," he told Raif as their makeshift raft wallowed in the passing waves and often threatened to roll completely over.

The night passed very slowly. Each minute seemed to drag into hours. Every time Jem looked over his shoulder at the moon, it seemed to be no closer to the far western horizon.

Sometime much later, the sea calmed some. The waves, which had looked more like mountains with sharp peaks, now smoothed out to gentle rolling hills of black water sliding beneath the raft.

Jem's right shoulder hurt more than the rest of him. He felt with his left hand at the place where the *Powderhorn*'s paddlewheel had ripped his shirt. It stung sharply to his touch, and he thought he could feel a deep cut.

He was wondering how badly he had been bleeding when Raif whispered, "Jem, I am not sure, but I think I just saw a shark swim by." Jem raised himself up enough to look where Raif was pointing. The moon cast pools of pale light dancing across the sea. At first he saw nothing, and then a dark fin sliced slowly through the water only a few feet away.

59

"Stay real still," Raif said. "Maybe he will not see us."

"He don't have to," Jem answered, "I'm bleedin' an' he smells it."

Raif groaned. "I should have known this was a bad idea, going with you." Even before his words were out, another fin appeared and then another. Something bumped the raft hard, nearly rolling it over as both boys scrambled to get farther out of the water.

The dark, shining body of a shark rolled in the water beside them, so close they could see the flash of his teeth and smell his rotten odor. Other fins appeared, cruising slowly and circling the raft. There was another bump, and both boys hung on for dear life.

"They are trying to shake us off. What are we going to do?" Raif wailed.

"Hold on!" was the only answer Jem could think of as another shark took a large bite out of the cotton bale beside him and swam off with a mouthful of cotton and burlap.

A strange, green glow streaked through the water below them. "What was that?" Raif gasped. Before anything else could be said, another flash passed directly under the cotton bale. It looked to Jem like some ghostly sea monster, a phantom snake with a glowing body. One second it was long, and the next, short and curling as it raced just below the surface. Even more frightening than the sharks, it sent chills up Jem's spine.

"They are sea serpents!" Raif cried and began to pray loudly in Spanish. Suddenly, the ghostly creatures were coming from every direction. Glowing green trails of light flashed through the waves, darting and circling until the sea glowed an electric green all around the raft.

Never had Jem seen or even heard of anything like it. Old sailors talked about sea serpents, those awful, mysterious creatures who were said to rise up out of the sea to eat ships and everyone on them. Jem always figured they were just wild stories, made up by sailors to scare landlubbers. Right now, he was not so sure.

He realized suddenly that the sharks were no longer attacking. All around him, he could hear strange breathing noises, like something he had heard before.

"Dolphins!" Jem yelled at the top of his lungs. "They're dolphins. I hear 'em breathing!"

"They do not look like any dolphins I ever saw," Raif answered doubtfully.

"That's 'cause we never seen 'em at night before. They're stirrin' up the water and makin' it glow, just like a ship does. And there ain't nothin' a dolphin hates worse'n sharks."

"Dolphins?" Raif asked, still not believing it.

"Yeah, dolphins. Look real close when one of them slows down. You can see their faces."

"Yes, yes, I see them! I think you are right. But why do they make that long, green trail?"

"I don't reckon anybody knows why a ship's wake glows at night sometimes, but it does, and this must be the same thing." A few of the dolphins stayed with them for the rest of the night, circling and playing around the cotton bale as it rose and fell, driven on the wind and steered by some uncharted current—to where, they did not know.

Dawn came very slowly. At sea, the last hours of the night are always the longest and coldest, even in the the middle of summer. Jem shivered as he watched the dimmer stars fade away. The eastern sky changed from black to deep purple, then pale blue and into a dozen shades of pink.

He could see the waves plainly now, row after row, marching steadily across the sea. The sun was a crimson ball of fire as it climbed over the horizon. Suddenly it was day, and Jem felt a little better.

"Now, if we just had a good breakfast," Raif grumbled.

Jem raised himself as high as he could and scanned the sea around him, hoping for some sign of ship or land. The cotton bale was becoming water-logged and floated very low in the water now. He saw nothing except the endless sea.

They heard the sound of breaking waves before they saw them. A dull, distant roar began to rise over the regular sloshing of water against their cotton bale.

"What is that?" Raif wanted to know. "It sounds like a storm is coming."

"Ain't no storm," Jem assured as again he rose up and looked around. Ahead of the raft was white water. "That's surf, and surf means we're almost on land!"

Raif also raised his head and looked around. "Then how come I can't see it?"

" 'Cause we're so low to the water, we can't see anything 'cept water." The cotton bale rose slowly on the back of a wave and picked up speed. "But we're fixin' ta feel it!"

They rode sluggishly over the white crest of the wave. As they slid down into the valley of water which followed, another wave broke behind them. White water boiled on its crest as it bore down.

"I think this one is gonna flip us!" Jem called over the roar of the surf. One end of the cotton bale hit bottom with a bone-jarring bump just as the following wave lifted the other. Jem found himself being pitched forward into the surf and carried forward by the breaking waves. His head went under and scraped on the bottom. Scrambling to his feet, he looked around and saw Raif beside him, just as another wave knocked them both down and pitched them onto the shore.

For a long time, Jem lay exhausted on the wet sand. As he slowly felt his strength returning, he struggled to his knees and looked around him. A deserted beach stretched out in both directions for as far as the eye could see. There was not a single tree in sight. Beyond the high-tide line, salt grass and sea oats grew among sand dunes which were bigger than those on Galveston Island.

Raif spit out sea water and said, *"Madre Maria*, this is the loneliest place I have ever seen."

Jem sifted a handful of sand between his fingers. It was different from the sand on Galveston Island, whiter and almost as fine as powder.

"I got a feelin' we're a real long way from home," he said.

10

The blistering midday sun burned on Jem's bare shoulders as he walked through ankle-deep sand. He wished now that he had not discarded his shirt so quickly last night in the water.

"I am so hungry that I am beginning to see little tortillas floating around in front of me," Raif moaned as they trudged up the side of another sand dune.

"Eatin' won't matter much if we don't find water," Jem answered. "We'll die of thirst long before we even think about starving ta death."

"I don't know," Raif said. "I am already thinking about starving to death."

Since dawn they had walked aimlessly along the deserted beach where they had been cast ashore. Except for the sea gulls which circled overhead and a few tiny sand crabs running along the beach, they had seen no other signs of life.

Away from the beach, there were higher sand dunes. They had decided to walk to them in hopes of seeing something more of where they were. But as they scanned the horizon from atop the highest dune they could find, they saw nothing encouraging.

To the south, the blue waters of the Gulf of Mexico stretched as far as the eye could see. Figuring from where the sun had risen, Jem decided that the shoreline was running about east and west. It looked as though it went on forever. Turning his eyes to the north, he saw more water, and then, far in the distance, a tiny brown thread of land.

"Reckon that's the mainland, way over there," he told Raif. "Most likely, we're out on some island that lays about like Galveston or Bolivar with a bay in between us and the mainland."

"I wonder if anyone lives out here?" Raif said, looking around him.

"Can't see why they would. There ain't nothin' here but sand."

"Uncle Moss told me about 300 Spaniards who got shipwrecked once, somewhere along this coast a real long time ago. One of 'em walked all the way to Mexico," Jem said.

"One of them? What did the rest of them do?"

"Got ate up by Injuns." Jem started down the dune, and Raif looked around one more time before following him.

They were almost to the beach when they stumbled onto a small tidal pool of sea water. The ocean had washed out a narrow cut across the beach, which let a little sea water become trapped behind the first line of sand dunes at each high tide. A few clumps of salt grass and sea oats grew on its banks. Large, blue crabs lurked just below the surface, and several brightly colored fish darted through the crystal clear water.

"If I could catch one of them," Raif said, licking his lips, "I think I could eat it raw."

"Reckon you'd have to," Jem answered, " 'cause we ain't got no way to cook it. 'Course, first thing we gotta do is figure out how ta catch one."

65

During the rest of the afternoon, they tried several ways to fish the tidal pool. Jem cut a strip of cloth off his pants leg and used it to tie his pocketknife to a stick he found on the beach. This he used as a spear. After an hour, though, he still had caught nothing. Raif tried using his shirt as a cast net and had a little better luck. He managed to catch one large, blue-green crab, which pinched his finger so hard that he dropped it back into the water.

By evening, their luck improved. It was Raif who first noticed that the pool was getting smaller.

"Yeah," Jem agreed. "The tide's running out and drainin' the pool, but some of the fish can't get out with it!"

An hour before sunset, only a few isolated puddles of water were left, and in one was a large, flopping redfish. Raif managed to grab it with his shirt and carry it proudly up on the bank. In a very few minutes, Jem had cut off its head, cleaned it, and scraped off most of the scales. He then cut it in half and handed one of the pieces to Raif.

"Raw fish," Raif said thoughtfully. "I have heard that in some places, people eat it all the time." With that, he bit down and ripped off a piece of the cold fish. He chewed hard, his face turned a little green, and Jem was sure he was going to vomit. Finally, he gulped down his bite, put his hand over his mouth as he swallowed, and took a deep breath.

"It tasted terrible," Raif burped.

Jem sniffed at his piece. It smelled disgusting, like something Uncle Moss's cat would eat. But he closed his eyes and put it slowly into his mouth. As he chewed on the tough, leathery fish, he decided that it tasted almost as bad as it smelled. His stomach turned over and tried to crawl up into his throat as he swallowed. To his surprise, he did not vomit, and he felt a little better, despite the taste.

"Seems like I ain't quite so thirsty now, either."

Raif agreed and took another bite. By the time the sun had set, nothing was left of their fish except the head and a few bones.

The wind came up after dark and cooled the night air. Jem and Raif remained by the tidal pool, somewhat protected from the wind. Sleep did not come easily on the hard sand. They took turns watching the ocean for any sign of a passing ship, although they had no idea how they would signal if they saw one.

Jem was dreaming about Talva when Raif awakened him. She had been calling to him from someplace very dark and far away. He had tried to answer, but his mouth would make no sounds. He had tried to run to her, but his legs seemed to move in slow motion and the wind pushed him farther and farther away.

"Jem, Jem, wake up!" Raif whispered loudly in his ear. "There is somebody or something out there. It is white and it was floating along the beach!"

Jem tried to shake the sleep from his mind as he sat up. The moon had risen while he was asleep, and now the whole scene was bathed in its light. Shadows moved on top of a sand dune. Two green, glowing eyes stared down at him.

"There it is. It is coming for us!" Raif exclaimed. Beside the two green eyes was a flash of white, fluttering in the wind. "Come on, Jem, run!"

Raif pulled him to his feet but Jem stood his ground. "No," he said. "I think it's all right." Then Getana barked and came bounding down the sand dune. Talva was with her, barefoot now, but still wearing her white dress. In the moonlight, it appeared to float on the wind as she ran toward them.

"Talva!" Raif shouted. "It is you! We thought you and Getana were dead!" Then suddenly they were all embracing and dancing around the tidal pool as Getana barked and frolicked with them in the moonlight.

"I am not certain just how I did survive," Talva admitted after the excitement of her arrival had died down. "I think part of the ship hit me when I dove. The next thing I remember, Getana was keeping me afloat. Later, we found one of the tables from the dining room floating nearby and we held on to it until we washed up on this shore."

Jem and Raif recounted their adventures with the sharks and the dolphins. "We ate a raw fish," Raif announced rather proudly when they had finished.

Talva nodded. "That is good. It will give you strength, and keep away the thirst, for a while at least."

"I saw the cut on the beach and suspected there might be a pool like this behind the dunes," Talva said.

"How come you were walking in the dark?" Jem asked.

"Before the moon rose, I thought I could see lights to the southwest. Of course, the moonlight would hide them now, if I really saw them at all."

"Maybe we should start walking now," Raif suggested, "while it is cool."

Talva shook her head. "I think we should rest. The tidal pool will supply us with food. Perhaps in the morning we can also find water."

Jem and Raif agreed, and so they all lay down close to Getana and slept restlessly as the incoming tide again filled the tidal pool.

When Jem awoke, the sun had already risen. Talva was kneeling beside the pool, using a stick to pull oysters out of the water. With Getana beside him, Raif was looking over the top of the nearest sand dune at something down on the beach. As Jem started to get up, Raif suddenly slid back down beside him.

"Jem," he said seriously. "You know how sometimes you think everything has gone wrong and nothing worse can happen?"

"You mean like now?" Jem grumbled.

"Yes, my friend, just like now. We have been thrown overboard, almost eaten by sharks, washed up on this deserted beach where we could very easily starve to death or die of thirst."

"Yeah, so what are you tryin' to say?"

"Well, my friend," Raif continued. "This morning, I did not think there was anything else really bad left to happen to us."

"So?"

"So, something else very bad just happened."

Before Jem could ask, Raif put his finger to his lips and motioned for Jem and Talva to follow him. Together they crawled up one of the sand dunes and peeked carefully over the top. There on the beach was a large figure lumbering aimlessly across the sand.

"Is that who I think it is?" Talva asked in a whisper.

Jem nodded. " 'Fraid so. Firewhiskers threw him overboard too."

"Maybe he'll just go on by," Raif said hopefully.

As they watched, Bruno stopped beside the washed-out area of the beach. For a long moment, he stared dumbly at the sand. "Bruno see feetprints," he mumbled. "Bruno see little bitty feetprints."

"They are mine, I fear," Talva whispered.

Bruno looked up toward the dunes and squinted his little, piglike eyes. "An dey go dat way. One little feetprints, two little feetprints, three little feetprints," he said as he started toward the dunes, stomping his own big, bare feet on top of each print as he walked.

11

"We are in real trouble now," Raif whispered as they watched Bruno carefully following Talva's footprints in the sand.

"I think not," said Talva. "In fact, Bruno may become just the friend we need."

"Friend?" Raif was whispering so loudly that Bruno stopped and looked around, listening. "You have been out in the sun much too long. Believe me, any big ape like that who throws me to the sharks is not my friend."

"Not yet. But I will reason with him."

"Reason with him? *Reason* with him? You may as well reason with a steamboat!"

Talva ignored him and stood up. "Bruno!" she called. "We are up here, all of us. We want to talk to you."

As Jem and Raif stood up also, a look of complete confusion spread over Bruno's face. He squinted both eyes and one corner of his mouth hung open. "Duh, I know you, little girl. You sick big bad dog on Bruno."

"Yes, Bruno, I sicked a big bad dog on you because you were going to hurt me and my friends," Talva answered, speaking very slowly so he would be sure to understand the first time.

Bruno shifted his eyes to Jem and Raif. "Bruno feed you to da fish, huh, huh. How you get here?"

"We washed ashore, just like you did," Jem called.

Bruno's eyes narrowed and he looked mean. "Bruno not like you. Now Bruno bust your heads good." He started toward them, his big feet churning up the sand like a small whirlwind. He was almost to the top of the sand dune before Getana sprang at him and her teeth snapped an inch from his nose. Bruno lost his balance, fell backward, and rolled head over heels back down onto the beach. When he finally managed to get to his feet, he saw Getana sitting calmly beside Talva.

"Bruno not like dogs," he said sadly.

"Your friends all betrayed you," Talva said. "You helped Firewhiskers take over the *Powderhorn*, and what did he do for you?" Bruno looked like he could not think of the answer, so Talva continued sternly. "He threw you to the sharks; that is what he did."

With his mouth drooped at the corners, Bruno sat back down on the sand. "Bruno thirsty, Bruno hungry, Bruno not have fun."

Talva walked confidently up to him. "Come," she said. "We have food, and if you help us, we may also be able to find water."

To everyone's surprise, Bruno got up and followed her to the tidal pool. With Jem's pocketknife, Talva opened one of the oysters and handed it to Bruno. "Here, eat this. In a little while we will catch some fish."

Bruno gulped down the oyster. Smacking his lips, he said, "Dat pretty good. You got more?"

"Two more, that is all. If you eat more, you will get sick."

Bruno gurgled as two more oysters slid down his throat. "Dose taste pretty good," he burped.

"Hey, Bruno?" Raif asked. "You have any idea where we are?"

Bruno nodded his head several times. "Sure Bruno know where we are. Dis is Texas, everybody know dat."

"Right, Bruno, we're in Texas," Raif sighed and shrugged his shoulders. "Well, I thought it was worth a try."

The sun was not yet very high, but already it was hot. "Did you say we could find water?" Jem asked.

Talva nodded. "Perhaps. Getana has found it for me before, on the islands near home." She pointed to Getana as the dog sniffed around the edges of the tidal pool. "She is as thirsty as we are." Talva went to her and petted her head. For a few minutes, they seemed to be talking to each other very quietly. Then Getana trotted off through the dunes, away from the beach.

They all followed, although Jem and Raif were careful to keep a safe distance between themselves and Bruno. Getana wandered aimlessly for a while, sniffing here and there. Presently she stopped at a low place between two sand dunes, where thick clumps of salt grass grew. She pawed the ground several times and then began to dig.

"I bet she digs up a bone," Raif said.

"And if she does, you'll probably eat it," Jem laughed.

"Be quiet and help her," Talva snapped and began digging beside the dog. Jem shrugged and also began to dig.

As the hole slowly became deeper, the sand began to change color. "It's damp," Jem announced, "and cool."

Bruno had been watching and now he said, "Bruno dig better dan dog." In a second, he had pushed Jem and Raif out of his way and was on his knees, digging furiously with both hands and throwing up a growing pile of damp sand. Talva also backed away and sat down.

For the rest of the morning, the digging went on. With only their hands to work with, it was a long, exhausting job. But the thought of water, real water which could keep them alive and take away the terrible parched feeling in their throats, drove them on.

73

By noontime, the hole was deep enough that Talva could stand up in it. "Give me your shirt," she said to Raif, who was now too tired even to ask why she wanted it. He just watched as Talva spread it out beside the hole and piled several handfuls of wet sand on top of it. She wrapped the shirt tightly around the sand and twisted it until the sand was compressed into a tight ball. Then she held it over Bruno's head.

"Open your mouth," she said. Bruno looked at her dumbly as she squeezed the sand inside the shirt until a few drops of water fell into his open mouth.

"Ummm . . . dat good," Bruno sighed. "Bruno think you nice little girl." He frowned at Jem and Raif. "Not sure 'bout dose guys."

They continued digging and squeezing a few drops of fresh water out of each handful of sand. Jem was amazed that, after drinking only a few drops, he no longer felt thirsty and again had the strength to keep digging. Another few hours passed before water was actually standing in the bottom of their hole.

"We must still strain it through a cloth to get the sand out," Talva announced. "But if we drink very slowly, there should be enough here for us all."

Later they caught more fish from the tidal pool. Bruno ate them whole and did not seem to care at all that they had not been cooked. Even Jem admitted, as he chewed on a tough piece of raw fish, that it did not taste quite as bad as it had last night.

As his strength returned, Jem once again began to think about all of the trouble that had landed them here on this deserted stretch of coast.

"Hey, Bruno," he asked at sunset. "You know where Firewhiskers is goin' with the *Powderhorn*?"

Bruno shook his head. "Firewhiskers no tell Bruno nothin'. He say he got big camp somewhere, big secret. He gonna put buncha cannons on duh big steamboat, den he be big pirate again, catch buncha ships, get buncha gold an' rum an'—"

74

"Bruno," Talva interrupted his rambling. "What do you know of the man who wore the tan suit? One of the men called him 'Thompson,' I think."

Bruno swallowed another fish. "Dat Mexico Thompson. Him crazy. Him bad crazy."

Talva rose suddenly and walked away from them, down onto the beach where the surf was crashing and sea gulls were circling in the twilight. Raif was dozing on the sand, and Bruno was sitting by the tidal pool watching two small fish.

As darkness settled around them, Jem rose tiredly to his feet and followed Talva down to the beach. He found her looking out to sea, with the tide lapping about her ankles.

"Why you so interested in Mexico Thompson?" he asked.

Talva continued to gaze out at the dark sea. "I do not know. I felt strange when I was with him, as if he were really two people, and one of those people I had known once before, somewhere very long ago. It is something I have never felt before and it confuses me. I cannot think right." She turned away, and for a while they walked in silence, down the beach as the waves played around their feet.

"Maybe you did know him once when you was real little, before your mother moved up on the bayou."

Talva's hand moved to the locket around her neck. "If it were not for this, I could almost believe that —"

Her sentence remained unfinished. She released the locket and pointed down the beach. "Jem, look! The lights!"

12

All day they walked west, along the burning sand beach which seemed to stretch on forever. Last night, after much argument, they had finally agreed that they must leave the tidal pool and the shallow well, even though these offered small amounts of food and water.

Talva had shown them the distant lights, a faint, flickering orange glow, far, far to the west. "There is not enough food or water here for all of us," she had insisted. "We should go now, for in a few days, we will all be too weak to walk."

Raif had argued against it. "Suppose that is an Indian camp. This kid does not want to find any more trouble."

"Looks too big ta be an Indian camp," Jem had said. "But that still don't make it no easier to walk away from the only water we've had in two days."

In the end, it had really been Bruno who made the final decision. "Bruno go see pretty lights," he had stated and started walking.

The afternoon sun sent heat waves rising from the sand and made the whole scene dance and shimmer as Jem strained his eyes in hopes of seeing something ahead.

His throat hurt and his tongue felt as if it had swelled up inside his mouth.

Beyond the beach, the dunes were larger, more like rolling hills with scattered patches of salt grass and creeping vines. Just on the other side of the tallest hills, there seemed to be a single tree, just barely sticking up over the top of a hill. As Jem looked again and blinked his tired eyes several times, he realized suddenly that it was not a tree at all, but the very top of a mast!

"A ship!" he called, pointing at the mast.

Beside him, Raif wilted with relief. "*Madre Maria*, when we get there, I am going to drink a whole barrel of water. So what are we waiting for? It is just over there a little ways. Come on!"

"Why would a ship be back there?" Talva asked.

"Reckon there's still a bay between us and the mainland, so it must be anchored in some cove," Jem said and started toward the dunes.

"It is certainly hard to see," Talva said, touching his arm and stopping him in his tracks.

Jem suddenly had a sick feeling. "Yeah. Maybe it's supposed to be hard to see."

"What are you talking about?" Raif sounded disgusted.

"Ben said they used ta hide ships up on Clear Lake 'cause the tall trees would hide the masts. Maybe this one is here so the hills will hide it."

"Yes, and if that is right, we should not be out here on the beach where we can be seen either," Talva said in a lowered voice. With Bruno following and keeping as low as possible, they crept forward. Only one small sand dune stood between them and the hill when they saw the first cannon.

Jem motioned for them all to take cover and then inched his way forward, up the low dune. Partway up the large hill was what he had at first thought was nothing more than a patch of tall salt grass. But now, as he raised his head carefully, he could plainly see a low wall of sand and earth, covered with sticks and grass. From behind it, the long, brass barrels of two cannons pointed out to sea. At least two men, heavily armed and dressed in ragged clothing, were dozing in the shade of the cannons.

As he watched, the afternoon sun flashed for a second off something higher on the hill. Jem slithered back until only his eyes were exposed above the dune. A man with a telescope pressed against his eye sat well hidden above the cannons and watched the blue waters of the Gulf.

Jem scrambled back down the hill to where his friends were waiting. Without a word, he signaled for them to follow and then led them back to a safe place among the dunes.

"Cannons?" Raif whispered when Jem told him what he had seen. "Are you thinking what I am thinking, that we have walked into Firewhiskers's camp?"

" 'Fraid so," Jem answered. "But we'll have ta get closer to tell for sure."

"Could it be anything else?" Talva asked.

"I don't see what. And, if it is his camp, that mast must belong to the *San Antonio*, and the *Powderhorn* must be back there somewhere too."

Carefully, they worked their way around behind the cannons and crawled to the top of another sand dune. Spread out before them, on the banks of a small cove, was an ugly city of makeshift tents and thatched huts. Several men in ragged clothes dozed beneath a lean-to made from driftwood and a sail. Nearby, a peg-legged sailor with a patch over one eye tended a cooking fire where a goat was being turned slowly on a spit. A few pigs wandered aimlessly about, rooting under the barrels and crates which lay scattered around in no apparent order.

On the camp's far side was a rough stockade, built of logs and guarded by two men. "That must be where they are keeping the passengers of the *Powderhorn*," Raif said.

In the cove, the *Powderhorn* lay anchored alongside the *San Antonio*. Black flags displaying skull and crossbones flew from each ship. Workmen were busy aboard both ships, and several longboats were pulling back and forth from shore. From aboard the *Powderhorn* came the sounds of saws and hammers. As they watched, a cannon was being lifted on ropes, over from the *San Antonio* to the steamboat's deck.

"They're mountin' guns on her," Jem whispered. "Reckon they're gonna use her for a pirate ship."

"*Madre Maria*, with a steamship like that, they will be able to catch any ship they want!"

"Bruno go bust Firewhiskers head now," the big man said and started to stand up.

"No, Bruno. Not now," Talva warned, grabbing at his shirt. "Later."

Bruno hesitated and then lay back down. "Duh, okay. Bruno wait. But Bruno getting pretty mad."

Raif was still looking at the ships. "I wonder how they got them into the bay?"

"Look yonder," Jem said. "There's a point of land farther west, and it looks like a pass into the ocean."

Talva added bitterly, "And through it, he can sail out and capture any ship which passes."

"We gotta try ta do somethin'."

"Before we do much of anything, we are going to have to find food and water," Raif insisted.

No one argued with that. They were all so weak they could barely walk, and their throats were as dry as sand.

"Let's find a safe place to rest 'til dark," Jem said as they slipped back, out of sight of the camp. "Then, me an' Raif will sneak up and try ta steal some food and water."

"Bruno come too. Get buncha rum."

"That is not a good idea, my hungry friend," Raif told him. "You are a little too big for sneaking around in the dark. You just wait here, and we'll bring you something good to eat, okay?"

Bruno nodded his big head slowly and followed them as they moved back among the endless miles of sand dunes.

It was well after dark before Jem and Raif prepared to sneak into the camp.

"I must come with you," Talva said as they started to go.

"No," Jem told her. "You better stay here with Bruno."

"Getana will stay with him. I must go."

Jem started to object again, but there had been a note in Talva's voice which told him it would do no good. "Okay, I reckon," he said and turned away.

Darkness covered their approach to the pirate camp, and they slipped easily up behind one of the tents. They ducked into the shadows as a half-dozen rough-looking men passed by, headed toward the center of the camp. A large fire was burning in front of the largest of the huts, and most of the men seemed to be gathered there. A fiddle squeaked out a lively sea chantey, and several drunken pirates were trying to dance a hornpipe. Wild laughter and curses rang in the night.

Talva tapped Jem's shoulder and pointed to a barrel a few yards away. "Water," she whispered and handed him an empty jug she had just picked up. It smelled like sour rum, but Jem took it anyway and darted over beside the water barrel. He felt in the dark until his hands found the wooden plug on its side and then carefully filled the jug until he felt the cool water run out over his hand. He could not resist splashing a little on his face before he replaced the plug and slipped back to where Talva was watching. They all took long drinks then, at last relieving their burning thirst.

Raif licked his lips when he had finished. "Now, if we can just find some food to go with this, I will be a very happy kid."

"Cooking fire was that way," Jem said, pointing toward the wild gathering in the camp's center. They moved closer, keeping to the shadows and among the tents and barrels. They were near the hindquarter of a goat, which lay by the fire when several pistol shots rang out from the camp's center. The shots were followed by more laughter, and then the crowd quieted down.

Jem raised his head slowly over the top of a barrel. He could see Firewhiskers standing on top of some boxes, with a smoking pistol in each hand.

"Brothers of the Coast!" he bellowed to the crowd gathered before him. "Ye be the filthiest pack o' sea dogs what ever sailed afore the flag of Billy Bones there." He waved one pistol in the direction of the pirate flags above the anchored ships, and a cheer went up from the crowd. "And ye be here ta witness the birth of a new and golden age!

"In just two days more, me hearties, we'll have a dozen cannon aboard the steamer there. Then we'll pounce upon every ship what dares ta sail this here coast." Another cheer rose above the crowd.

"It'll be like the old days were," Firewhiskers continued to rant and rave, "when Henry Jennings ruled New Providence Island an' gave safe harbor to every scallywag what plundered the Spanish Main from Cartagena ta Madagascar!

"With those ships and 200 of these here newfangled Colt guns," he brandished one of the five-shot revolvers, "we'll rule this coast. We'll take all the ships, we'll ransom the towns, just like Morgan did at Porto Bello!"

Firewhiskers slobbered in his beard as the men roared their approval. "We'll send word to all our scattered brethren ta join us here until we've got a pirate navy that no one dares cross."

"We heard Lafitte's men are coming!" a single voice called from the crowd.

Firewhiskers roared with laughter. "Aye, and they be welcome! Once Mr. Thompson here settles his score

81

with Lafitte, they'll join us!" He pointed at Thompson, who was leaning against a barrel. He now wore a loose shirt with billowing sleeves and a wide belt which supported a rapier and his two revolvers. His hat was pushed far back on his head. He showed no expression as the crowd grumbled restlessly.

At the mention of Thompson's name, Talva raised herself high enough to see him just as he turned away from the crowd and disappeared into the darkness. "I will join you later," she whispered and started to move.

Jem grabbed her arm. "No! Don't . . . not now anyway."

Anger flashed in her eyes, and Jem thought that she would pull away from him and go. But her anger passed; she released a long-held breath and nodded.

"We'll find out, somehow. I promise," Jem said.

Firewhiskers seemed to have finished his speech and the crowd was starting to drift away from the fire. "We've stayed too long now, we better get outta here. Where's Raif?"

"Over there," Talva answered after looking around. Raif was by the cooking fire, struggling to remove a whole, barbecued goat. As they watched, he hoisted it over his shoulder and then picked up the hindquarter, with his free hand. He ran toward them with all of it.

"They're gonna miss a whole danged goat! Why'd ya go and take so much?" Jem asked angrily as Raif handed him the hindquarter to carry.

"So much?" Raif panted. "The little piece may be enough for us, but we have to feed Bruno too."

Jem could not argue with that. Footsteps rustled not far away, and the three quickly started making their way back out of the camp.

Mexico Thompson stepped into the light of the cooking fire. He walked carefully to where the goat had been cooking and looked with interest at the small footprints in the sand. He knelt on one knee, examined them closely, and noted the direction in which they led.

Coals from the cooking fire stirred suddenly to life. Sparks swirled in the air and embers glowed brightly. The sea wind combed through his hair and moaned softly —a sad, mournful sigh. He raised his eyes slowly up to the night sky as the moon was just touching the sand hills.

"Must you haunt me now," he whispered, "now, when the end is so near?"

13

"But there's gotta be somethin' we can do ta stop 'em," Jem insisted with his mouth full of roasted goat.

"The only thing we can do to stop those pirates," Raif said, "is to find a way to get a message to Galveston, or maybe someway to the United States Navy."

"Jem," Talva spoke quietly, "if we took one of their longboats and sailed it across the bay to the mainland, how far do you think we would be from the nearest settlement?"

Jem tried to picture a map of the Texas coast in his mind. Galveston Island was about thirty miles long. At the west end was Pass San Luis. There had been small settlements there from time to time, but he did not think anyone lived there now.

Beyond Pass San Luis was Follett's Island, another long, narrow strip of land. It was cut by a pass at the mouth of the Brazos River, and there was a settlement there. But, judging from the *Powderhorn*'s speed, Jem was afraid that they were even farther south than that, probably cast ashore somewhere along the miles and miles of uncharted seashore known as the Matagorda Peninsula.

"Near as I can figure, we'd probably be a hard fifty miles from the nearest town," he said.

"And what if we took a longboat and sailed out into the ocean? How long would it take us to reach Galveston or Indianola?"

"Hard ta say with a sailboat. It all depends on how the wind blows. I reckon Indianola ain't more'n a day or so south. Galveston would probably take longer."

Raif swallowed another mouthful of goat. "There are just two little tiny problems with that plan. First, I do not think Firewhiskers is going to give us one of his longboats. And second, if we just happen to get lucky and steal one, he has a very fast steamboat and also a very fast schooner to catch us with."

Jem knew he was right. There was only one way the plan could work. "Well, I guess we just gotta sink his ships then."

"Can we do that?" Talva asked.

"Maybe not by ourselves," Jem looked at Bruno, who had swallowed an entire leg of goat and licked his lips. "But we got Bruno."

"*Madre Maria*," Raif sighed, "he ate the whole goat."

Bruno burped so loud that it echoed among the dunes. "Bruno bust ol' Firewhiskers' boat, duh huh. Bust 'um real good."

So they made their plans and rested all that day in the shade of a few scraggly cedar trees a mile or so from the camp. They all knew that, if the plan worked, this might well be the only rest they would get for a very long time.

It was late, and the moon was high before the pirate camp finally quieted down for the night. Keeping to the dunes, they skirted the tents and stayed close to the bay until they reached a point on the cove where the two anchored ships lay between them and the camp. Jem was relieved to see the dark outline of a longboat moored at

85

the *Powderhorn*'s stern as he waded into the dark, blood-warm water. His toes squinched in the soft, sandy bottom as he waded across the shallows. With each step, the water got deeper until only his head and shoulders remained above the surface. At last, he could wade no farther and struck out swimming toward the *Powderhorn*'s silhouette.

There was something very scary about swimming in the dark, Jem thought as he reached out to touch one of the *Powderhorn*'s paddlewheels. It was slippery and slimy with seaweed as he pulled himself up onto it. But inside of the paddlewheel was a maze of spokes and braces, nicely placed for climbing. Although they too were slick, Jem had figured that this would be the easiest place to sneak aboard.

The top half of the paddlewheel was covered by a huge, wooden shroud with "*Powderhorn*" painted on the side. The smells of dead sea life mingled with those of grease and oil as he climbed carefully in the darkness, making sure that he had a firm grip with one hand before moving the other. The ship creaked and groaned, and the paddlewheel moved a few inches. At the paddlewheel's hub was a short catwalk and a door leading out onto the deck. Jem opened it a few inches and carefully looked around. A few lanterns were burning along the main deck, but everything seemed still.

Raif and Talva climbed silently up beside him, but there was some noise on the paddlewheel below. "I wish that we could have found someplace to leave Getana," Raif whispered. "They are making too much noise down there."

Below, they could hear Bruno muttering as he climbed with Getana on his shoulders. "Nice doggie now, not bite Bruno. Bruno take you up on big boat. Be nice doggie."

Jem slipped out onto the deck and pressed himself against the cabin wall. "C'mon," he whispered, "let's get to the engine room."

"Are we not going to wait for Bruno?" Raif asked.

Jem shook his head. "He's comin'. We can move quieter without him." Neither Raif nor Talva answered, but both darted quickly over beside him, and together, they started moving carefully toward the engine room.

They were passing the main salon when a door opened suddenly behind them and the light of a cabin lamp flooded onto the deck. They spun around to see a big, bad-smelling man with a cutlass in one hand and a pistol in the other towering over them.

"Well, blast me eyes, three of the biggest little bilge rats I ever seen, sneakin' around. Fish bait, they looks like ta me!" The cutlass was raised over his head when Bruno tapped him on the shoulder. The man stopped in midair. A confused look spread over his unshaven face as he saw Bruno looking down at him.

"Dat not nice!" Bruno said and brought his fist down on top of the man's head. Jem managed to catch the cutlass as the pirate dropped it and collapsed into Bruno's arms, but his pistol rattled on the deck.

"Hey, Bruno," Raif said, "that was pretty good."

"Quick, drag him back into the salon before somebody else sees us," Jem ordered, picking up the pistol.

Inside the salon, everything was a mess. Most of the fine furnishings were gone, and two cannons now sat where some of the tables had been. In the center were several small kegs marked "gunpowder." Beside them was a stack of small wooden boxes, each one about two feet long. "It looks like he was supposed to be guarding these," Raif whispered as he examined one of the boxes. "I wonder what is inside?"

With Raif's help, he used the cutlass to pry the lid off one of the boxes. Inside, packed in a neat row, were twelve Colt revolvers. Jem lifted one carefully in his hand; its shiny black metal finish felt cool and heavy to his touch. Carved into the wooden handgrips was a single five-pointed star, the Lone Star of the Republic of Texas. These were the guns, Jem knew, which had belonged to the Texas Navy, the guns which Commodore Moore had carried so proudly aboard the *Austin* and *Wharton* at the Battle of Campeche just last year. Now they were needed just as badly by the Texas Rangers. He would not feel right about destroying them.

"We can take 'em with us!" he announced excitedly. "The longboat's big enough."

"That is crazy!" Raif protested. "There are at least fifteen boxes here. It will take too long to carry all these boxes back to the stern. We are going to be lucky if we can just sink the ship and get out of here."

"Bruno'll help. He can carry two or three at a time."

Raif shook his head, but Jem looked at him and said, "Raif, we gotta try!"

Raif looked hopefully at Talva, but she only nodded her head in agreement with Jem.

"*Madre Maria,*" Raif said, almost to himself. "When we started out tonight, I thought we had a very silly plan. Three little kids, a dog, and a mountain with ears were going to swim out here and sink two pirate ships. But now, I think that was a pretty good plan—at least when you compare it with this one, where we take all these guns, load them into the longboat, and then sink the ships." He grabbed one of the boxes. "Well, come on, do not just stand there. Let's get this silly plan over with."

Jem and Raif, it was found, could each carry one box of pistols. Bruno managed three easily. Talva went ahead of them and scouted their route, back to the *Powderhorn's* stern where they had seen the longboat moored. Jem was almost surprised when she told him that the coast was clear.

They figured that it would take three trips to load all fifteen cases of pistols aboard the longboat. They had made two trips without interruption, and Jem and Bruno had already started back for the last load. Talva was about to help Raif load the box he was carrying when she stopped suddenly and looked off into the distance.

"Come on, Talva, give me a hand," Raif whispered as he struggled with the box in the longboat's bow. "Talva?"

"I must go," she said in a strange, faraway voice.

Raif was getting mad. "Of course you have to go. We have to get out of here just as fast as we can."

"You must all leave quickly. Keep Getana and do not wait for me. I will return if I can." With those words, she turned and started forward.

Raif scrambled after her. "You cannot do that!" he whispered loudly and grabbed at her arm.

She turned on him in a flash. "Do not even think of trying to stop me!" Her voice was hard and threatening as she pointed her finger at him.

Raif took a couple of steps backward. Specks of green fire danced in her eyes. Her white dress flowed about her in the night breeze until it looked almost as if she were floating. And then she faded into the shadows.

14

Mexico Thompson drew both of his revolvers as he stepped out of the *Powderhorn*'s darkened wheelhouse. The night wind brushed at the sleeves of his shirt and sent strange chills down his spine. There was a presence carried on the wind, and for days it had been growing stronger.

He took the stairs down to the cabin deck slowly, one silent step at a time. Cautiously, he looked down the long row of cabins, all quiet and empty. He moved aft then, and took another set of stairs down to the main deck. Lamps were burning low in the salon where the cases of revolvers and gunpowder were stored. The guard should be somewhere near.

From a distance, he saw the door hanging open and knew there was trouble. He quickened his pace and pressed himself against the wall beside the open door. Once again he checked both of his pistols, took a deep breath, and rushed into the salon.

The guard lay on the floor—out cold. The kegs of gunpowder were still there, but the cases of revolvers were all gone.

"The longboat," Thompson muttered. He turned and started for the door, then stopped dead in his tracks. A small figure in a white dress stood in the doorway.

"Talva," Thompson's voice wavered. "Have you come to haunt me again?"

"I have come to learn the truth," she answered, stepping inside. "Who are you?"

"You don't know?"

"What my heart feels, my mind will not accept."

Thompson sighed and laid his pistols on a table. "I do not believe you would have learned the truth, had you been able to go on to Indianola. For if there are records of your birth there, I know nothing of it." He sank tiredly into one of the salon chairs. "Somewhere in New Orleans are the church records of the marriage of Regina Gray to Capt. Thomas Thompson, master of the Mexican schooner of war *Correo de Mejico*. . . . But wait—I must start at the beginning."

"Just tell me why you left her." Talva demanded bitterly as the tears on her cheeks glistened in the flickering light.

"Please hear me out," Thompson pleaded quietly. "I told you of the War of 1812. But what I did not tell you was that I lost my ship to a French privateer named Jean Lafitte. And I was wounded in a duel with him just afterward. I left the English Navy in disgrace."

"I know that," Talva said.

"Regina and I were married when I was offered a commission in the Mexican Navy. My ship was assigned to blockade duty on the Texas coast, and this proud new captain wanted his bride near. Galveston was already restless. I moved Regina to the village of Texana, up the Lavaca River. It seemed like the safest place at the time."

Talva started to say something, but Thompson raised his hand. "As you most probably know, the revolution came, Mexico lost, and Mexico Thompson could not come home."

91

"But they said you changed sides, helped some Texian sailors escape from prison."

Thompson nodded. "And by then, Regina Gray Thompson had vanished."

He rose and slipped the pistols back into his belt. "Texana had been burned to the ground during the 'Runaway Scrape.' I searched for her all along this coast. In Galveston there was some talk of a woman who had been accused of witchcraft, but no one knew, or cared, where she had gone.

"And so, finally I returned to New Orleans, thinking she might have gone back there," he said as he paced to the far wall and then turned suddenly. "She had been quite famous there, you know."

"No," Talva answered. "She never spoke of it."

" 'Madame Regina,' she was called, the 'sorceress of Barataria.' Her shop on Bourbon Street made beautiful jewelry, but in her chambers behind, she told the fortunes of some of the most famous men and women in that city."

Talva touched the locket, still hanging around her neck. But her next question went unanswered as Thompson continued. "Of you, dear Talva, I knew nothing. Oh, you are her daughter; there can be no doubt. Your face, your hair, your speech, your every movement tells me that you are Regina's daughter." He paused and turned away from her, taking a deep breath. "But if I am your father, I have no knowledge of it."

"Do not lie to me!" Talva cried, choking on her tears. "Do you think that the daughter of so famous a sorceress does not know when she is being lied to?"

Behind her, the door was suddenly kicked open. Talva spun around as Firewhiskers, flanked by two men, burst into the salon. A fourth man entered from the other side with a musket in his hands.

"Thompson, ye lunatic!" the pirate growled behind his red beard. "What in the name of Davy Jones is goin' on here?" Talva backed away from him as he strode in rolling steps across the salon. "You," he pointed a hairy finger with two gold rings on it at Talva's nose. "You should have been a midnight snack for some hungry shark. How'd you get here?"

Talva said nothing and moved closer to Thompson. Firewhiskers's eyes darted quickly around the room. "The guns!" he roared. "They're gone!"

"Quite so," Thompson remarked dryly and pointed to the unconscious guard. "The fool you left to guard them seems to have hurt himself somehow. Rather clumsy of him, I say."

"And you be standin' here, doin' nothin about it?" Firewhiskers raged. "You're ten times the trouble you be worth, Thompson," he hissed between clenched teeth. Then a crooked smile spread across his bearded face. "I don't need you anymore, Thompson. I got the ship you helped me take, and I got the secret anchorage you found." His eyes moved to the man behind Thompson, and his head nodded.

The musket was raised and leveled at Thompson's back before he could turn. "No!" Talva screamed and raised her hand, pointing at the man's eyes. The weapon did not fire. Talva's body trembled and her eyes glowed in the dim light. Blue fire danced along her arm and sparks jumped at her fingertips. The musket rattled on the floor, and the man clutched at his forehead with both hands, screaming as he ran out onto the deck.

Firewhiskers's eyes were the size of saucers. "Quick, shoot the girl!" he cursed as he drew two pistols from his belt.

As Talva turned to face Firewhiskers, the night exploded. Three pistols fired at the same time. Smoke and hot gases hit her face and stirred her hair, but all she saw was Thompson's back as he faced the three pirates.

For a brief moment, there was a ringing silence. "Why?" Firewhiskers said as he stared at Thompson, wrapped in a vale of drifting powder smoke.

Thompson staggered backward and almost fell. Then he regained his balance and cocked both his revolvers. Blood trickled from his lip as a smile spread across his lean face. "She is my daughter," he said evenly and fired until both guns were empty.

15

"What do mean, she just ran off? You shoulda stopped her!" Jem exclaimed as Raif excitedly told him what Talva had done. They were in the *Powderhorn*'s engine room and Jem was holding a lantern for Bruno. As they spoke, Bruno happily swung his sledge hammer and broke one of the valves which fed sea water to the steam engine. A fountain two feet high sprang up as the valve shattered and splashed on their legs.

"Stop her? Ha! That is easy for you to say," Raif exploded in Jem's face. "She has gone all *loco* crazy. You just wait. When she looks at you and her eyes start glowing like a cat in the dark, she will do what she wants to do!"

Jem pushed past him. "We gotta find—" he started, but then a scream, distant and chilling, echoed through the ship. A moment later, they heard the shots.

With Raif close behind, Jem sprinted out of the engine room and ran blindly forward along the deck. Without slowing down, he burst recklessly into the salon and almost tripped over the body of Firewhiskers, sprawled in the doorway.

Mexico Thompson lay on the floor, his head cradled in Talva's lap as she pressed a piece of tablecloth against his bloody shirt.

"The locket," Thompson was saying in a voice so weak that Jem could barely hear. "It was Regina who made them, cast them all with the symbol of the falcon. As I said, she told the fortunes of the most famous men in New Orleans. Among them were the Lafitte brothers. She spied for them, used her powers to warn them whenever there was trouble."

"But she left all of that, to be with you," Talva said.

Raif pulled on Jem's sleeve. "The camp is getting all stirred up, and there are a lot of boats heading this way. They are going to get here in time to stop the ship from sinking."

Jem tried to force his mind to reason with the new danger, but there seemed to be no answer.

"Come on, Jem," Raif was pleading. "What are we going to do?"

It was Thompson who spoke. "Take the longboat and get away from here." He nodded his head toward the stack of powder kegs. "Break open one of those and pour me out a fuse," he smiled grimly. "There will be no ship left to chase anyone."

"No," Talva insisted desperately, "you will go with us. Come on. Help me move him!"

Thompson raised his left arm painfully, touched her cheek, and forced her to look into his eyes. "We both know that even you cannot make that happen."

"I won't leave you," Talva cried.

Jem turned to Raif. "You and Bruno take the longboat out, away from the ships. Watch for us. We'll swim to you."

Raif looked very pale. "Be careful, my friend," he said as he hurried out. Jem crossed the room and pulled the wooden stopper out of one of the powder kegs. A trail of gray powder spilled onto the floor as he carried the keg to a spot near where Thompson lay. He then let the rest of its contents fall into a pile around the other kegs. Raif appeared at the doorway about the time Jem was finished.

Jem looked up, surprised and worried. "I thought you went with Bruno. What happened?"

Raif gave him a sheepish grin and shrugged. "I sent Bruno with the longboat. I thought I better stay here and keep you two out of trouble."

Jem looked at him for a long moment. "Thanks," he said simply. "Now, let's get outta here." He turned to where Talva was still kneeling beside Thompson. "We gotta go."

"It is too late," Talva said in a distant voice as she closed Thompson's eyelids with her fingertips. "He is dead."

Jem could hear shouting in the distance. There were several dull thuds as the first of the boats from shore reached the *Powderhorn*'s stern. He picked up one of the oil lamps burning nearby. "Come on, Talva!" he tried to say calmly.

She rose slowly, as if nothing mattered, and walked to where Jem was standing. "Give me the lamp," she said. "I will do it."

She held the lamp close to Thompson's face. In death, Jem thought, he looked very peaceful, as if the losses and failures of a lifetime had suddenly all been taken away.

"Her spirit lives along the bayous," Talva whispered to her father's ear. "She walks with the forest deer and flies with the gulls. She rides with the dolphins and wades the shallows with the shorebirds. She loved you very much. Go now, and be with her."

The lamp shattered and flames licked across the wooden floor. Gray smoke fizzled and hissed as they found the end of the powder train.

Jem took Talva's hand and, together with Raif, they ran for all they were worth, out of the salon and forward along the deck. Shouts and curses echoed behind them as the pirates swarmed, like angry ants, onto the ship.

On the foredeck, the gangplank was sticking out over the bow and hoisted at a slight angle. Without slowing down, they ran to its end and jumped.

The *Powderhorn* exploded behind them. The salon walls blew out, and soon the lower deck dissolved into a ball of burning orange. Her smokestacks toppled. Both bow and stern rose up out of the water as she broke in half and vanished into a cloud of smoke and steam.

Sparks and burning debris sprayed across the *San Antonio*'s nearby deck as well. Flames soon burst to life in her furled sails, and in a few minutes she also was engulfed in a whirlwind of fire.

The noise of the blast left a ringing in Jem's ears which kept him from hearing anything for a long time. Burning pieces of the ship fell all around them as they swam as fast as they could, away from the inferno. As the ringing died away, the next thing he heard was Getana's barking. Just ahead, the big dog was standing in the bow of the longboat as Bruno rowed toward them.

Totally exhausted, they managed to climb aboard with Bruno's help. For a while, they all lay there, watching the fires blaze in the distance and consume the last remains of the two ships.

"We gotta get some sail up and get out of here," Jem said finally as he staggered to his feet. Again, with Bruno doing most of the work, they stepped the longboat's stubby mast and hoisted the small lug sail. Jem took the tiller and pointed the boat toward where he thought the pass out into the Gulf of Mexico should be.

From the dunes, there were several flashes of light. A split second later, a rumble like rolling thunder echoed across the bay.

"Why are the cannons firing?" Raif asked. Before anyone could give him an answer, there were three more flashes directly ahead of them followed by the sharp reports of as many cannon.

" 'Cause there's another ship runnin' in through the pass!"

They all looked ahead, and there, silhouetted against the night sky, was the black outline of a ship sailing toward them. More cannon fired as she raked the pirate shore batteries with a rolling broadside. As Jem steered away from the oncoming ship, he could see that she was a schooner, long and low to the water with raked masts and a long bowsprit. White water boiled around her knife-like bow as she ran in through the pass under jibs and topsails.

"Duh uh," Bruno said. "We in big trouble now."

"I don't think so," Jem answered, remembering a night last spring at Rollover Pass when his father had boarded a dark ship, just like this one, and sailed off into the night. "That's the *Pride!*" he shouted, standing up at the tiller.

"I hope they don't shoot us by mistake," Raif said as Jem turned the longboat toward the *Pride*'s dark outline.

"Better get up on the bow and let 'em know who we are."

Raif was just beginning to move when a musket ball sent splinters flying from the longboat's mast. Bruno stood up and roared in his loudest voice, "Hey! No shoot at Bruno. Me good guy now!"

16

The *Pride* rode nervously at anchor in the cove with her sails loosely furled and her guns still loaded and run out. Lookouts clung to the fighting tops of both her main and mizzen masts. Constantly they searched the horizon with long telescopes for any sign of sail or smoke, for the *Pride* remained a ship without a country and, despite whatever had happened last night, she would still meet no friends along this coast.

At sunrise the wind began to freshen out of the southwest. Jem pulled the blanket closer around his shoulders and stared out over the quarterdeck rail. There was no trace of the *San Antonio*. Only a few wisps of black smoke still drifted from the charred remains of the *Powderhorn*. Her blackened engine and machinery lay like a skeleton, half-submerged in the bay. Ashore, where the pirate camp had been, the *Pride*'s longboats were preparing to ferry out the first of the *Powderhorn*'s passengers.

Jem's eyes wandered up into the *Pride*'s tall rigging, where the United States flag flew from her main gaff.

"We keep a lot of flags aboard," Lafitte explained as he too eyed the U.S. colors. "Under these conditions, it is best that the passengers believe they have been rescued by the United States Navy." With a sly smile, he brushed a bit of dust from the blue American Navy captain's coat he wore and straightened the gold-trimmed, cocked hat. "With a little luck, we can masquerade as a revenue cutter long enough to land them all safely at Galveston."

"What ya gonna do with all them Colt revolvers?"

"Jack Hayes of the Texas Rangers is an old associate of mine. I'll see that they are delivered. With all of the trouble he is having with Indians, I am sure he will be very happy to get them."

A longboat had come alongside as they talked, and now Bruno was coming aboard, carrying a barrel on each shoulder.

"Can ya take Bruno with you?" Jem asked. "He works real good, but he'll just get in trouble again if he goes back ta Galveston."

His father nodded thoughtfully. "He seems to be fitting in quite well. If he wants to join the crew, I'm sure we can find a place for him, for a while, at least."

Jem left the quarterdeck then and made the long walk forward, past the masts and the cannons. He smiled as he passed an open hatch and could hear Raif below decks, talking to the cook. He sounded like he had his mouth full. Jem climbed the stairs to the small forecastle were Talva was standing alone, looking out at the remains of the *Powderhorn*. There was a blanket around her shoulders too, and her hair hung in a mess of damp tangles.

"I'm sorry 'bout your father. Can't nobody say he wasn't a real brave man," Jem said awkwardly. For a long time, she did not answer or even seem to notice that he was beside her. When at last she did turn to look at him, her tears had dried in dirty streaks across her face.

"You told me something once, very long ago, on a morning much like this. You said that it does not matter where someone comes from. The only thing that is really important is where they are going." Her lips trembled in a weak smile. "You were right."

From the quarterdeck, Lafitte watched them, standing together on the bow as the *Pride* prepared to make sail. "Strange," he said to himself, "that after all these years, two of Regina's lockets should come home." He turned his eyes to the distant, blue horizon. A faint, sad smile spread across his weathered face. "Could it be that someday, we shall see one more of them?"